Ba-Ya Play Cook

An anthology of Short Stories

Zuleka Dauda

Forte Publishing

Monrovia. Virginia. Bangkok.

First Published in 2021
Published by:

FORTE Publications
#12 Ashmun Street
Snapper Hill
Monrovia, Liberia
[+231] 88-110-6177

FORTE Publishing
7202 Tavenner Lane
208 Alexandria
VA, 22306

FORTE Press
76 Sarasit Road
Ban Pong, 70110
Ratchaburi, Thailand
[+66] 85-824-4382

fortepublishing@gmail.com

This book or any portion thereof may not be reproduced or used in any manner whatsoever without the expressed written permission of the publisher except for the use of brief quotations in a book review.

Cover Photo Credit: Samuel Aboh Jr.
Printed in the United States of America.
Copyright © 2021 ZULEKA DAUDA
All rights reserved.
ISBN-13: 9798707953392

Dedication:

For the children of Liberia who were child soldiers
forced to suppress their memories,
For the young girls masking their fears and insecurities
under the label "big jues",
For the sexual abuse and rape victims forced to settle
things the family way and
every other child that still lives through the experiences
that we fail to address. I see you. The world will hear about
you. These stories are for you

Author's notes

These are real stories roughly based on real people. The only things I've changed are the names and places. If I did not experience it, I know someone who did or someone who told someone who then told another someone and that's how that goes. The idea is to tell these stories and expose that we continue to rob our children of their innocence. Impunity for rape and other violence remained prevalent in Liberia. Mama Liberia is resilient, but we must acknowledge our wrongdoings and work to correct them. We owe it to the most vulnerable among us, the Children.

Zuleka

*Thank you to my mother and sister
for allowing me to be a child.*

Contents

Ba-Ya (Play Cook) 1

The Family Way 11

Small Pekin 18

Fine Bright Geh 28

Big Jue 40

New Normal 48

My Owna Kinja (Burden) 58

Uncle ECOMOG 64

About the Author 73

Ba-Ya (Play Cook)

Growing up, we used to love cooking. Mercy would bring most of the ingredients from her house and I'll bring the coal pot and cooking spoons. Tanneh would join us sometimes, but mostly play cooking time was for Mercy and me. Behind the house, near the burgorbor hill, was where we usually cooked. The burgorbor hill was a little reddish mound where termite colonies lived. The bugs that came out were tasty when you added salt and roasted them. Additionally, the hill made for the perfect spot to hide and do our play cooking from time to time.

Ba-Ya was our secret cooking club. It was only for us children. We were the cooks, tasters, the critics, and everything. We just wanted to do what we saw the adults do, but they never approve of it. We had to keep our ingredients, processes and cooking a secret. It felt good cooking and knowing that at any moment we could get caught and possibly spanked. The thrill kept us going. After all, it was our little cooking club.

Mercy and I would plan the meal for each week on Sunday evenings. We made time to decide on the ingredients, which we would gather during the week and carefully hide them in holes in the mud hill until it was time to cook. Although what we cooked depended on what was available to grab in Mercy's house, it still felt exciting every time we could scrap together things to make a full meal. The leftovers made for some very interesting renditions of the typical Liberian meal. If we didn't have something we would just substitute or *remix* it as we used to say.

It really didn't matter what it was, we'd have fried beans instead of the red oil beans or use Torborgee oil to cook cassava leaf, all in the name of our own remix.

"Po ley deh mehn, la our own remix." Mercy would say.

"La remix bisnis we comin' run our stomay?" I'll answer with laughter.

We had a system where we rotated who got to cook the soup and who was stuck with just the boring rice. A Liberian meal without rice is certainly not complete. We liked joking that even as heavy as fufu is, we still had to eat rice as a real Liberian did.

Cooking rice was always the easy part, so none of us really liked doing it. All one did was simply add water and maybe a little salt and wait for the rice to cook. There was really no interesting part of tasting involved in cooking rice. Now, the soup, hmmm, that is where all the fun was. My favorite soup to prepare was palm butter. It was so much work but in all the mess, there was enough flavor to surpass any other soup.

There's this song we sang, *"palm butter rice too sweet, you eat it, you want some more"*. Indeed palm butter was succulent. It is the juices from palm nuts with the wonderful magic of Maggi cubes and other seasonings. I liked to think of myself as the palm butter champion! Mercy knew I was better at it than she was, so she always sat back and watched me cook it.

First, I washed the palm nuts (while chewing on one or two of the raw ones). Next, I would boil the palm nuts, to soften the skin. The boiled nuts then had to be pounded in a mortar. Since we didn't have our own

Ba-Ya (Play Cook)

mortar, we used a big stone to crush the palm nuts. Mercy used to clean that stone constantly to avoid sand in our meals.

It was a whole process to watch and I took my time with each step. Along the way, I picked and ate whatever scraps that fell or left on the spoon.

After crushing the nuts, thus effectively removing the skin (which gives the juices that make the butter) I'd then strain it. This meant I had to pour water through the mixture to separate the palm skin from the crushed body and creating the butter. The strainer we used was a piece we tore off the net of the aluminum window screen of Mercy's parents' home. If they ever found out, we might never cook again but that was part of our process.

The thick red mixture after straining and separating is the raw part of the palm butter that I'd begin the cooking with. Our pots were old mixed vegetable cans or some other tin cans that we made work. We made do with whatever we could to complete our kitchen. For me, the best part about cooking was tasting. Although I also enjoyed stirring the pot, adding seasoning and meat or whatever scraps we found to call meat. Sometimes we got leftover dried fish, pig foot, or other random parts of the chicken. Other times, we just threw in wild mushrooms growing on the side of the houses and that was the meat.

Palm Butter has this rich beautiful orange-red coloring. I loved looking at it while it was boiling. Although sitting and watching was the hard part because we were anxious to eat the finished product, it was harder waiting and hoping an adult would not walk by and stop us from cooking or throw out our entire kitchen! The anxiety during the wait was all worth it once we made it to the end.

"Food na done ooooo!" I would say to prepare Mercy to get the spoons or whatever utensils we could lay our hands-on.

Once, our entire kitchen got thrown right out into the trash without hesitation. We did not see that coming and it all happened so fast. We lost our utensils and just about everything else. Our pots were old kidney beans cans, the mortar was the large rock and the pestle another rock. We would constantly have sand in our meals (when Mercy hurriedly cleaned the rock), but who cared? I recall that a well was within walking distance from where we cooked so we fetched water to wash our food sometimes, but in all seriousness, I think the sand was part of our ingredients. What mattered was, to us, the food tasted good.

The adults said they threw away our things to protect us from burning ourselves. I don't believe them. They were just jealous. However, every time they did, we still managed to get our kitchen back in order, though it was hard getting everything back.

We had a small coal pot made from scrap metal we collected from the dumpsite. My brother Eddie-boy worked in the welding shop with a Guinea-Kpelle man named Sekou. I offered to do his chores for a few weekends just to convince him to make us a small pot for our cooking. But he refused, calling our cooking, "behind-the-house cooking" and complained that I would get him into trouble for making it since we had been warned numerous times by the adults to stop our cooking. He reminded me of what mother used to say. "La foolishness yor lor be on, one day yor wey bwehn yorseh," "If yor bwehn, nobody carrying yor to hospital'. Eventually, adding washing of his school socks to doing his chores, made all the complaints go away and we got our coal pot.

We didn't cook to feed ourselves; it was just to make time go by and keep us happy. We enjoyed practicing how to cook. I imagined I was my mother when I stirred our little cans of soup. Our little "behind-the-house-cooking" was all about doing what the adults did in the real kitchen. It was our own version of what we thought real cooking was. We all knew

Ba-Ya (Play Cook)

that if we got caught, they would punish us, but the few times we got to complete our cooking were worth all the risks.

Some other kids cooked using sand as rice, and other random leaves as stew. The red hibiscus was a popular favorite because of the smell and slippery texture similar to the Liberian dish Palava sauce. They could not really eat them when they cooked. For them, it was all about the process. But, we were not other kids. We wanted the real thing, so we gathered the real leftovers and ate whatever mess we made.

One time, we made some really salty potatoes greens. I swear I could feel my tongue slowly swelling from the salt, but we still ate it. No other ingredient in the sauce that day came close to the amount of salt we had in it. But, this was all part of the Ba-Ya process.

Another time, Mercy mistook sugar for salt and we had ourselves a over sweetened Liberian-style gravy. We laughed as we ate our way through the sugary pieces of dried bony fish we dropped in the gravy for flavor. I did not know what flavor meant, but I used it a lot when we play cooked.

"Add la one der for flavor," I would say about anything going in the pot.

"Keep some of the bony dirt for flavor oooo." Mercy would say.

My mother used to add seasoning in a funny way; she'd knock her palms together when brushing off the salt (but it sounded like clapping) with the remaining salt falling off her hands into the soup. But I knew she was just adding more seasoning so I also incorporated that into our cooking.

At home, we didn't have a real kitchen like at Mercy's, but I knew what a real kitchen looked like. A real kitchen had a sink to wash dishes and pour the water in it after you washed the rice. In my house, we washed the dishes in a big plastic dishpan and wasted the water behind the house on the grass. In real kitchens, there are wooden cabinets that hold dishes, seasoning, and pots. For us, we kept our pots, pans, and utensils under the bed. We kept many of our things under the bed as storage and to make room for us at night. Living in a single room meant we had to get creative with space. We didn't have much, but we made it work.

Mercy and her family had a lot of things and a much bigger house. I love reading about things I knew I would only find at her house, like refrigerators, VHS, satellite dish, throw pillows, and area rugs. I used to think things in books were only for people with money. I could never relate to the things I read about. What my family had was everything that was outside of books.

Mercy and I didn't need a real kitchen, because cooking kept our friendship strong. When we were not cooking we talked about cooking. When we were not talking about cooking, we made plans to do so. Our friendship revolved around cooking.

We were in the same grade, but my family could not afford the Catholic school Mercy attended. Our other friend Tanneh lived closer to Mercy's house and attended the same Catholic school, but was one grade ahead of us. She was smarter and taller than we were. I did not like Tanneh, but I wanted to be like her. I remembered at Mercy's 9th birthday party last year, Tanneh called us strange for always playing with fire and cooking "strange food" near the burgorbor hill. After that, we stopped inviting Tanneh to our cooking sessions, but she showed up uninvited sometimes. She just stood there with judgmental looks and never ate our food.

One afternoon, during a random drop-in visit from Tanneh at our cooking site, we heard someone calling out her name from inside of Mercy's house. I was leaning over our makeshift table crushing the peppers for our soup that day. The voice coming from the house sounded like a man so I thought it had to be one of Mercy's brothers.

"Tanneh, ehn I calling you," the voice came again.

I was right that it was Mercy's older brother. Everyone called him Bishop, but his real name was Snortee. Mercy had two older brothers. Snortee was the younger, but always the loudest. He usually made his presence known from miles away even before you saw him. If he was not talking loudly,

Ba-Ya (Play Cook)

he wore a lot of cologne - quite hard to miss; or he will sometimes put colors in his hair like bright pink or purple. Nobody could mistake Snortee for his older brother Duke. Duke was the calm, older brother whom everybody admired, barely interacted with and rarely saw. Mercy used to say that even in her sleep, she could tell which brother was doing what.

When Snortee called Tanneh that day, we thought nothing of it. In fact, I was glad she did not have to stand there and give our cooking those ugly stares. Knowing how she felt about our cooking, I just wanted her gone.

She made her way into the house and we continued cooking in peace. Mercy sighed with relief that she didn't have an extra pair of eyes watching her every move as she was on soup duty that day. I added more coal to the fire and went to fetch a plastic bag to use as a cover for the rice, like I saw the adults do sometimes. I've seen older women, towards the end of their cooking, cover their rice with plastic bags so I assume even the plastic added flavor!

I found a black plastic bag near the well. We called these black plastic bags *mind-your-business* bags. There is something secretive about them, but also, they make for strong carrying bags. So, I took the bag to the well and rinsed it out before heading back to our site near the burgorbor hill. The bag was too big for rice in a can, but I would keep the rest for another day. As I was making my way back trying to rip a piece of the mind-your-business bag, I saw Mercy motioning towards me to hurry. I doubled up my steps while shaking the water from the pieces of the plastic bag.

"Come yeh sometin," Mercy said.

"La wuttin."

"You na hearing that?" She asked standing right under the window of her own house.

I could hear heavy breathing and what sounded like crying. Mercy tried to peak, but she couldn't reach the screen on the windows. The windows had iron bars outside and a screen on the inside to deter burglars. Our little hands could not pull our bodies high enough to see what was happening inside. No matter how unusual the noise coming from inside was, we both knew it had to be Snortee. I heard him, but I also heard someone else.

"La who?" I whispered

Mercy put her fingers over my mouth to silence me. She ran to grab a block to help us get a better look through the window. I stood there hearing the soft cries under Snortee's breathing. He was loud as always. Through his breathing, he was saying something that sounded like 'wait' or 'way'. I could barely recognize which. When Mercy got back, the block was not much help. We still had no clear view of the room so this time I ran to get a chair from the front porch of Mercy's house. By the time I got to the porch where Mercy and her family usually sit in the evenings, I saw Tanneh holding tight to the collar of her dress and crying as she exited the house. I hurried towards her, but she made her way right past me.

"Tanneh, wha' happen?" I yelled behind her.

Tanneh did not stop crying or running. She went towards her house and didn't look back. I went back to Mercy in my confusion. She was still on the concrete block at the window where I left her. The smell of our food danced in the air with bewilderment.

"Tanneh wor crying ooo." I finally said

From where she stood, Mercy could see Tanneh run from the house. I knew she saw her too, but I had to share.

"Yeah, Ia her and Snortee wor inside there." She said with a grin on her face.

I must have missed something. Snortee and Tanneh in a room and she left crying. Mercy was not as shocked as I was. She was grinning. She got down from the block and returned to our cooking. I asked about what she said and that is when she told me calmly that it was not the first time.

"I na hear it plenty times when girls go in my brother dem room."

Ba-Ya (Play Cook)

She said, "La how dey can do, when our parents are out. Both of my brothers can bring girls dem in their rooms to be doing la thing with the same noise we jeh heard.

"Bor ha you know la Tanneh?" I asked.

"Snortee na bring Tanneh before," she confessed.

"Ah! Bor Tanneh wor crying ooo. Maybe she na like it."

"Sometimes, the other girls be crying too ooo. I na even hear dem say God and Jesus name when Snortee be doing rude-rude things to them."

"Rude -rude things?" I asked.

"Yeah, la how Snortee can call it. He like smor smor girls like us ooo. I na see Kumba, and some of the geh dem from our school in his room too," she confided in me.

I stood there shocked and jealous. "Snortee liked all the girls, what about me?" I thought to myself while stirring the ground pea (peanuts) soup. I looked around in case someone else could hear what we were talking about. Not too long after, Snortee came out of the house with his shirt hanging over his shoulders. He was his regular appalling self; making his presence known and whistling loudly as he walked away from the house.

We finished the rest of our cooking in silence. I barely had an appetite to eat that day. When we finished, we put out the fire, washed the dishes and returned them to our hiding spot for the next day.

I thought about what happened that day for the rest of the evening and into the night. I wanted to know more about *rude-rude things* but didn't want to get us into trouble. Mercy warned me to keep it between us.

Laying on our mattress, on the floor of our small room, I could still hear Tanneh faint cry under Snortee's obnoxious moaning and breathing. He must have been hurting her. He had to have been. I know I heard "wait" and that must have been coming from her. It sounded almost like an accusation instead of pleading. Tanneh always seemed so sure about everything. Even when she was picking on other kids, she was sure of herself. I remembered when she called our cooking strange, she didn't even blink or shrug. I wish I'd argue or said something back, but I didn't. I felt she was always so sure of herself so...

I thought maybe if she really wanted Snortee to stop, she would just say it and not plead. Or maybe she was really in pain? I felt bad for Tanneh. I wish we could say something, but Mercy was right, we could not tell anyone about this. In fact, Mercy said it was not new so maybe all the adults already knew about this. It was not our place to say anything. It was not even our place to play cook behind the house. If we wanted to keep playing Ba-Ya, we had to keep this to ourselves. After all, main ingredient of Ba-Ya is the secret of it all. This was a secret club.

The Family Way

"Let's just handle this thing the family way," Pastor Varney said. "There is no need to get this out of the family. We do not need to bring shame to the family by airing our dirty laundry." This was strange when one considers that even the pastor was a stranger, but only the church could know.

Staring into the distance, one thing was certain; I didn't want any part of it. I wish she never told me. My heart was heavy about all of this, but I'm glad it is no longer just between us. My conscience kept me up most nights, worrying about her.

Growing up, our parents always told us to protect each other. I used to fight for her in school. I even got suspended because of my fights for her. I protected her every chance I got.

However, this time, it felt different. I was protecting her secret and not her. I wanted to do more, but she didn't want me to do so. She just wanted me to let it be, but how? She didn't want to talk about it and protection meant just that-never talking about it. But how could I? Fed up with the impasse, I sought help. I brought in the church and for that, she hated me.

A while back, my Pa started being hard on us. He wanted us to excel in school so he hired a tutor. We already had a study class at the school following regular school hours. He took the TV from our rooms, reduced our allowances and even stopped our friends from visiting during the week. Sundays were for studying and preparing for the new week. The maid did the ironing and food preparation, so all we had to do was study and mentally prepare for the school week. My Pa ignored us mostly but made his presence known by the silence when he was around. He was a short, stubby man. When he wasn't yelling his way through the house, he was brooding as someone with so much on his mind.

Papa was an accountant for an insurance company owned by a foreigner. Many businesses in Liberia are foreign owned. Ever since the war, Liberians are the workers and foreigners are their bosses.

Papa's boss seemed like a nice man, but every time I hear my father talk about him, it was "Foolish Hassan this" and "Foolish Hassan that". Papa loved his job, but judging from his numerous complaints, one couldn't tell.

Sometimes he stayed in his home office all day on Sundays and only came out to use the restroom. My Ma would bring his food to the room and tell us he had a big project or the auditors were coming to their company. I always loved the house on those days. I didn't have to tiptoe in the living room or look over my shoulders when I played in the yard.

Mama didn't care as long as we stayed inside the fence. She was my favorite parent. She was there, but barely present on most days. It was as if she was just occupying a space or playing a part in a play. I never had to worry about her yelling or reducing our allowance. She moved slow and hardly ever got angry.

Once she yelled at the gate boy, but that was only because he kept calling her big Ma. My Ma hated titles. Liberian society is all about titles and positions. Things were more like, "Tell me your title or where you work, and I'll tell you what class you belong to." There are only two classes; the haves plenty and the not getting any! Society thrives off the back of poor people. The more money one gets, the more maids or house helps one gets. People will have a maid, a gate boy, a driver, a cook, a security guard, and even someone just to iron the clothes. Interestingly, having all this does not mean that one was rich. This is just how things were.

Labor was so cheap. Most workers made under $100 US. In our house, there was not much to do, but we had helps. This was my father's way of helping people from his village. We are Grebo people. My father spoke the Grebo language, but not when we were around. He never taught us and left no room to ask why. . My father grew up in Maryland County, but that was a long time ago. Maryland is the most southeastern point of Liberia. In a country where transportation to several parts can be challenging, coming to the big cities is a huge feat.

He prides himself on coming to the city and never returning. He said he wanted to make a better life for us. He speaks of the village life as something he escaped. He said that one day he would take us to see where he grew up. I doubt my father will ever do. But I am glad he offers the hope that I can one day see where he grew up and get to know a bit about my culture.

Sometimes I think we are losing our culture, but Papa doesn't think so. For instance, my native name is Dwe it means strong orwith strength and power. There is a whole story about my name, but Papa only said I was a strong baby. Papa is tightlipped about a lot of his culture. He is so adamant about leaving it in our past. Imagine he doesn't even use my Dwe name, although it is in my passport. He would rather use my "kwi" or as our people say, the civilized name- Michael.

Speaking of names, my mother often quarrel with the gate boy because she prefers to be called by her name.

"Silly Goat, stop calling me boss lady boss, lady- you hard to hear ehn?" she yelled.

Mama had one of those names that sounded like the ones in movies. Her name is Rachel. She is from the Kru tribe, but her family sent her to live in Monrovia at an early age. My father said during their school days, he enjoyed hearing her name when the teacher would do attendance. They both attended boarding school together.

Back then, when a family takes a child in, they gave the child the family's name as well. The Congau people or Americo-Liberians usually took indigenous children. This accounts for the loss of the family names for many people who then took on names like Thomas, Johnson, and Woods. My father loves those names. He said it helps you stay away from tribalism.

"Tribal names will jeh point you to the identity of a person. If yor name Janjay, people know straight you Bassa geh." he said.

"So my Dwe name la pointing to Grebo?" I asked him before.

"La it there oooo." He ended it as if it was a matter of fact.

My father didn't explain a lot of these things. He just said them and they were law. He was a man of very little words, but he meant them. I wish he would sometimes be more like my mother. She was so easy to talk to and treated people with so much respect. She talked to the house-helps with kindness. She looked people in the eyes and was never too busy. I always wanted her around, but not my father. I recall that he sometimes took business trips to neighboring Cote d'Ivoire and how those were the best few days. We stayed up late, ran outside in the rain, got midnight snacks, visited our friends, etc. There was a sense of freedom in his absence.

During one of his trips, my mother even played in the rain with us. She ran out to get us to stop but ended up staying. We laughed at her chasing us. We called out her name and ran around in circles. She even looked happier that day than when father was around.

I wondered sometimes what they talked about when they were alone. His favorite thing to say to her was "Thank you, darling". He said this often when she served him she gave him his morning tea, handed him his briefcase, served him his dinner, handed him his newspaper/TV remote, etc. she was always right there when he needed her. She was on time with his every need. She wore beautiful long house-gowns he bought from markets in Cote d'Ivoire She smiled gracefully when she served him. I could never read her. I was always searching for her face as I did the day we talked it "the family way".

The living room was crowded. My pastor, father, mother, my mother's oldest sister, visiting from the states, me, and of course, my sister all gathered. The room was thick with emotion. My little sister, whose bloodshot eyes bulged, was afraid. Sadness weighed her as she hung her head. I wanted to just reach over for her and hug her as tight as I could. The rest of us, except mother, were either angry and or consumed with fear. I searched all over her beautiful oval face but saw nothing. She just sat there expressionless, in a green, house gown with yellow embroidery on the neck and sleeves.

My Sister was smart, funny and creative. She could make anything out of the wax African fabric. She didn't need a sewing machine to make her own clothing. People at school copied her style. She never followed anyone and I admired her for that. I'd noticed her breasts were forming on her chest and she finally saw her period, but she was still a baby. The older girls told her she was a woman now. I overheard our housemaid tell her to stay away from boys. Whatever happened, I just never saw her as a woman. She was just my baby sister that lived down the hall from me.

My mother often went for church related activities. During a weekend while she was away for a revival, my father crept into my sister's room and forced his way on top of my sister. He raped her. He repeated it the next night and then the following night right before my mother's return. After my sister told me, I swore I'd kill him. I even dreamt about the ways I'd do it. Some nights, I'd see myself with my pillow in my hands slowly covering his face. Other times, I'd go to the kitchen to get something sharp to kill him. I wanted to eliminate him from our lives.

My sister cried for two weeks straight. She walked a funny way for the first few days. She stopped eating, she ignored everyone. She told me only because I wasn't a fool. I saw my father when he crept into her room the last night before my mother returned. I immediately suspected something, and my sister's behavior only confirmed it. My Father was an animal. How could he sleep with his own daughter? He never talked to her or looked at her when I was around.

I was her big brother and her protector, but I could not protect her this time. How could I? I was only the son of the man that harmed her. As we sat in our living room listening to him yell about his actions, calling it blasphemy and denying what my sister said about him. He called her a liar. I cursed him under my breath. I hated myself for being his offspring. I wanted so much to be bigger than him so I could crush his head in.

My sister would never lie about a thing like that I knew her. She was never good at telling a lie. When she told a lie, the side of her mouth curved in. I knew she was telling the truth.

It hurt that I had to hear her tell that story again. I didn't need to hear it from her again, but they made her tell us what happened. She cried as she told the horror of having our father forced himself on her. She lost her voice as she repeated what he said each night, "let me do it so it doesn't hurt when someone else does it". She told me it hurt. She told me he was heavy, but lay on top the entire time. He raped her Thursday, Friday and Saturday before our mother returned. He raped his own daughter and went back to his regular life of saying "thank you darling" to my mother on Sundays.

In that living room, he told a story of being a good man. He used big words to talk about the accusations. He called it an abomination and forbid my sister to speak his name with such a thing. He said children are known to have wild imaginations and even hallucinations. The pastor suggested we pray about the demons that wanted to divide our family. They always blamed demons for bad things. I knew the only demon in the room that day was yelling and calling my sister names. He was my own blood.

At one point, I told him I hated him and I hope he died. My aunt told me to never speak to my father that way again. The pastor wanted peace and continued to blame the devil. My mother was lost in her thoughts. I wanted her to yell. I wanted the reaction she gave the gate-boy for calling her "Big Ma". I wanted more from her than I had ever wanted. I know I love her barely-there personality, but I needed her that day. I wanted the fury that they talk about when they say "hell hath no fury like a scorned woman". I wanted her to be scorned! But the only person pouring out her soul in tears was my sister.

Then after about an hour of hearing what happened and listening to my father deny it all, the pastor suggested we handle it the "family way". This usually meant sweep it under the rug and pick up where we left. This meant going back to calling the monster papa and getting no reaction from my mother. Life as we knew it will have to go back to normal. No one outside of that meeting would know. As our people say, Kukujumuku, "You na inside, you na know". Not this time. I made plans to leave and not without my sister.

Small Pekin

That morning it was heavily raining. I always loved the sound of rain on our zinc roof. Sometimes when it rained this hard, it sounded like gunshots.

Oh, not those again! I was only eight years old when the last Civil War erupted, but I still remember it like yesterday. In my mind, I can still see the blood-stained sidewalks from where they dragged the lifeless bodies of innocent people. Sometimes, when I inhale fresh air, I am reminded of the stench of those days. During the war, taking a bath was a luxury, so people usually smelled like a mixture of old football boots and rotten eggs. The Liberian war will continue to dwell in the peripheral of my life.

That is why, the rain on the zinc that morning sounded like bullets in the distance. I saw the rebels far away in the distance or sometimes they were really close that I could see their heads through our bathroom window. They were always shooting it seemed. The bullets, however, were always quite loud to my scared little 8-year-old ears.

Liberia is situated on the west coast of Africa with her capital, Monrovia named after a former American President, James Monroe. My parents used to say Monrovia was not too populated, but since the war, it felt like rush hour traffic every single day.

Small Pekin

That morning of the rain was a weekday and the rain from the previous night had flooded parts of our bedroom. I did not attend school because my uniform was under the pile of wet clothes. I was one of three children living with my parents in our one-bedroom. The house had seven and a half rooms, but we only occupied one. I said seven and a half because the half room was actually a storage closet or pantry, but our greedy landlord rented it to a pehn-pehn (motorbike) boy name Moses.

In a war-stricken country like Liberia, people will do anything to maximize profit. People in their desperate attempts to make a living will invent a way when there was none. The room was no more than 20 inches depth and about 70 inches tall. Moses was about 5'4" tall. He had broad shoulders and muscles from lifting bricks when he would help out on construction sites to make extra cash. He could barely stand in the room and only had a mat on the floor where he slept.

As a pehn-pehn boy, he barely stayed in that tiny room, as he had to use his bike for transportation, kind of like a taxi man, but with a bike. This is how he provided for his baby and teen girlfriend who lived somewhere in central Monrovia.

The house was located in Dwazon, about an hour outside of Monrovia. There were other families in the other bedrooms, but my family occupied a room on the far right end. When you entered the house, there was a long hallway with rooms on each side and the tiny room attached to the back like a shed.

My father sold gasoline out of 5-gallon containers right on the main road. He sold mostly to bike boys in small, used, mayonnaise jars called pwen-pwen. These were easier to sell as bike boys came around more often.

My mother sold in the general food market. Sometimes she sold fresh pepper and other days, she dried the remaining fish, seasoned with pepper and sold it to the girls roasting fresh fish on the sidewalk. There were times when she had nothing at all, as business was not always good. She was a hardworking woman, but hard work does not bring wealth. I've seen her walk for miles, fight with drivers about carrying her goods, negotiate with retailers, come home and get right into mama mode- cooking and cleaning and taking care of us. She did it all, but we still barely got by.

I was the only boy of the children, although the youngest, I did most of the chores. In the mornings, I helped my father carry out his gasoline containers to sell by the roadside. He set it up on a stool, with a funnel to pour out the fuel into the bikes. I also had to fetch water from the nearby hand-pump and iron our school uniforms before heading to school.

My older sister, Sia was our cook. She usually warmed the cold rice before we left for school. Although we referred to leftover food as cold rice, Sia still had to wake up and make a fire to heat up the food for our breakfast. She was the artist of the family, always singing as she gathered the coal in the metal coal pot early in the mornings.

Kumba, the little one, sometimes helped me with fetching the water after she was done sweeping and cleaning the house. When I say house, please keep in mind we had just a room. The space felt as big as any house would. We partitioned the room with the old brown suitcase my father got from the Lebanese businessman that used to live near our house.

The suitcase was the landmark for the sitting area and the sleeping area. A small bench in the corner held our kitchenware. From the door, the suitcase sat slightly to the left with the mattress on the floor to the right. My mother and father slept on the mattress with Kumba, while Sia and I slept on a red mat near the door. When we would lay on the mat, the room door could not open, so we usually went to bed after everyone else.

Small Pekin

My mother kept all of our "good things" in a blue barrel near the window. Good things were church clothes, my father's radio, three drinking glasses and two plates that we never brought out to use, not even with strangers, and other things that were just hidden for whatever reason my parents had.

The roof of the room had a small leak so we kept our clothing in bags closer to my parent's mattress during the rainy season. The sitting area had two chairs made from rattan and a table covered with a crocheted blanket. The rest of the floor was plastered, but there was a piece of the rug at the entrance of the room to trap dirt from under our slippers. Sometimes, the room felt big enough when everyone was outside. Most times, we were cramped over each other with the smell of my father's gasoline between us.

The wooden windows opened to the outside letting in a nice breeze from the plum trees outside. Most mornings when we first open the window, since all the families did their cooking in the big kitchen outside, the sweet aroma came rushing through the window, only to be ruin by gasoline.

The rainy morning, my mother had already left for the market carrying Kumba with her. Sia and I stayed in the house completing some chores. We couldn't go to school in such heavy rain so at least, we had to help out with cleaning the mess from the rain. I took out some of the soaked items to the long hallway that divided the rooms. Sia was in the outside kitchen heating up the leftover Torborgee from the day before. Torborgee is made from bitter-balls and red palm oil. For most people, it can be bitter, but not me and my little belly. I was hoping that maybe she would give me some of the crust. I always loved the crust, because as the remainder of the food, it was full of all the spices! I was moving swiftly with my chores to get to Sia and remind her to keep the crust for me.

Zuleka Dauda

Ma Martha (pronounced, Matter) who lived right across from our room, came out as I was moving the plastic bag that held my father's old newspapers and other books. We usually kept old papers to help start the fire for cooking, but my father's newspaper collection was out of the question. He always read them before bed using our green kerosene lantern. Sometimes he left it burning until the kerosene ran out.

I used to admire him from my mat on the floor while I wondered what interesting stories he read from those papers. I was only in the 4th grade and enjoyed reading, but we didn't get assignments in newspapers. I love when our teacher sometimes called on me to do readings from the blackboard. One day, I hoped to be a teacher too and help my father and mother. I wanted to be able to buy my father a new newspaper every day so he didn't have to read the old ones repeatedly.

As soon as I brought the old papers in the plastic bag to the hallway, Ma Matter smiled at me from behind the green screen on her door. She motioned for me to come into her room. I placed the bag on the floor, near our door and walked towards her room.

As I entered, she closed the main door. Their room was across from ours. Her screen door was usually ajar which made it easy to see directly into her room, but I never really got a real look at everything until that day. Standing there, I saw the mattress was rested on a wooden bed. She had many teddy bears on her bed and a blue mosquito net hanging over it. There was a yellow and green plastic bucket in the corner of the room and her colorful curtain flying as the breeze made its way into her window. As I got closer, she stepped back into her room and said, "Come insah!"

Ma Matter was the wife of our greedy landlord. He smelled of cigarettes and usually sat under the plum trees playing checkers with his older brother. The gossip of the community is that he stole Ma Matter from his brother. His brother was always the nice one in my opinion. He didn't smell of cigarettes and never yelled about rent money or about noises when we played football in the yard. Sometimes I wish he was the landlord.

Ma Matter's husband was not in the room that day and the rain kept them from playing checkers. He must have been somewhere far. I went deeper into the room.

As she sat on the bed, she instructed me, "Put the hook behind the door!"

I did and turned around. I was looking around at all the things they had in their room. It looked a lot bigger than ours looked and had a lot more things in it.

A big brown TV set sat near a cupboard that held a lot of drinking glasses in it. 'What do you do with a TV in a place with no electricity?' I wondered. The room smelled of cigarettes just like her husband. There were more teddy bears over the TV set as well. The middle of the floor had a giant rug with a black and white square. The rest of the floor had a plastic mat with red lines running through them. There were wooden shelves in the far end of the room carrying clothes, shoes, and several of belts.

Ma Matter always went to church on Sundays. She was the best dressed in the church and probably the entire community. She had a raspy voice and walked strange. She asked, "Where your sister eh?"

"In lay kitchen." I offered.

She then tapped the spot of the bed next to her and said, "Come here mehn, why you sticking to dat wall?"

I froze.

Tapping the spot, again, next to where she sat, she insisted "Come, I way na bite you".

I've always helped Ma Matter carry her market bag from the main road into the house. I usually stopped right at the door and she took it from there. I've never been alone and this close to her. When I sat next to her, the bed felt soft. It made a funny squeaky noise. I wanted to apologize, but Ma Matter interrupted asking, "You sure you locked dat door?"

"Yes," I mouthed and shook my head.

She walked over to check and secure the hook on the back on the main door before coming back to sit next to me. Without warning, she reached over and touched my trouser zipper. I was astonished but smiled shyly as I dropped my head in shame. I was not wearing any briefs under my trousers. I only had three pairs of briefs and wore them to school or church. Ma Matter asked me, "Why you nah wearing briefs?"

"Oh, sorry." I laughed nervously and apologized.

She assured me by touching my face and pulling me closer to her. This time the bed was louder than before.

Ma Matter was fat. She had a huge butt that bounced like a football when she walked. Maybe that's why she walked so strange. My body stiffened when she pulled me.

She said, "Open it!" and pointed to my zipper. My hands nervously opened my trouser revealing my Toto. We refer to penises as Toto and vaginas as Tata. It is easier to talk about body parts when they sound friendly. At least that's what I think. Ma Matter laughed at the size of my Toto and said, "You nah man yet". In dismay, I covered my Toto with my hands.

She grabbed the collar of my shirt and stood me up, in front of her, with just one hand. She raised my hand from my trouser to her body. Then she asked me, "You nah touch woman before?"

I had not. Recently, my friends and I would spy on the girls bathing in the outside bathroom, which was actually a shack behind the house, made with aluminum-zinc and sticks. The zinc had some holes in them so we peeked through to see the girls using their dipping cups to splash water over their soapy bodies. It was the most exhilarating thing I'd ever done in my 12 years of life. If we ever got caught, no amount of begging would stop the beating the adults would give us. Yet, we stood our silly little bodies behind the zinc, watched, and giggled!

Ma Matter's body did not make me giggle. It felt soft but terrifying. I pulled back a little as she pressed my hands on a breast. Then she said, "Let me teach you." I love learning, but this was not something I wanted to learn. I didn't know why she chose me. I don't even know who told her I loved to learn, but here she was teaching me "woman business". This was a business too fast to understand. One minute you're cleaning up the mess from the rain, the next you're standing facing Ma Matter with your hands on her body. Things were moving way too fast.

I prayed someone would notice I was gone. I could hear voices outside, but people were dealing with the mess from the rain. I had to deal with this alone. Sia was probably stirring the Torborgee as Ma Matter took my hand and placed it under her dress.

She pulled my hand so far under, I had to drop to my knees. She smiled and said, "Stay there." She opened her legs to make room for me to kneel before her. The rain, it seems, which was still falling, chose to play a mimicking prank on me. It was falling as I fell to my knees. It poured harder as my heart raced faster; oh, it pelted our zinc and destroyed our living space as my innocence was being destroyed.

Oblivious to everything happening to me, Ma Matter guided my hands between her legs. I felt her panties, something hairy, then something moist, as she motioned my hands up and down. I just stayed on my knees moving my hands where she took it. She was laughing and said "You trying; now, put your mouth there!"

"Ehn?" I asked confused at her demand.

"Put yor mouth where yor hand air mehn," she said laying with her head back and looking at the ceilings.

Zuleka Dauda

I hesitated, but had no choice as her thighs were already squeezing my head between her fat, dark, hairy, under parts. I wanted to be brave, but I was scared. I wanted to pee. I also wanted someone to come in and see what she was doing to me or me to her. But, nobody came. Nobody saw. It went on until something dropped outside on the roof. It was loud enough to make Ma Matter push my head away from between her thighs and pull her dress down. She shooed me away quickly. I got up, wiped my mouth and ran for the door. I didn't look back, but I heard her when she said, "Da me and you secret you hear?"

I picked up the plastic bag right where I left it. I made my way quickly to the Kitchen. My sister came out carrying a cooking spoon. She didn't seem concerned nor bothered by my disappearance. She walked right past me into the long hallway. I stood there in the kitchen for a while; staring into the air, trying to collect my senses. It all happened so fast. I knew it happened, but did anyone else? I wasn't sure how long it lasted. The rain continued to make sounds, like the beating of distant ceremonial drums, on the zinc of the outside kitchen. The winds shook the branches as some green plums fell on the ground under the trees. There were puddles of water in spots around the yard. I looked around for signs that I was not alone.

There were none!

That evening when the rain stopped and my family was back into our room preparing for bed, I told them. I started by saying, "Ma Matter called me into her room today and locked the door.

My older sister laughed. "What?"

My father asked me, "Could you hand me the newspaper bag?"

My mother folded her lappa (African Fabric) and rolled it up to use as a pillow but said nothing.

Small Pekin

I spoke up again, this time saying, "Ma Matter brought me into her room, locked the door and started humbucking (bothering) me."

My father simply opened the newspaper to begin his evening reading. Again, my mother didn't say a word.

Sia, lying next to me, still laughing only said, "Small Pekin like you. You belleh shut up!"

Fine Bright Geh

We called her Yellow. She was my best friend. I didn't know why they called her yellow, because she did not appear to be yellow. I know they called me names because I was really dark, but Yellow just did not fit her description, really.

When we did colors in primary school, we all learned how to spell Yellow's name, although it was not her real name. Everyone called her that; even our teachers. As for me, they called me Blackie. I had other names like Darkness, Fire Coal, Burn, Night, etc… Mostly, family called me those names. I remember my Aunty TahTah calling me *Night,* but with such affection that I actually came to like the name.

In school, when Yellow and I would play, the kids would say, "Satan and Jesus dah best friends." I was 'black' and supposed to be Satan because he represented darkness. Yellow was *bright,* as we say in Liberia, so she represents Jesus.

A poster of Jesus that hung in the church and it almost looked like Jesus could be Yellow's father. I understood the references the kids made connecting my darkness to the evil men in Nigerian movies. The ones that wore horns on their heads, drew white circles around their eyes and made black magic using blood. By

Fine Bright Geh

extension, I surmised that I was dark like them and maybe I was evil.

As we grew up, Yellow got all the attention. Boys I liked would come to me and tell me they like my "fine, bright friend". With time, I didn't take it personally because I was used to it. Yellow got all the boys and I got to hear all the stories because we were quite close. I was her best friend. When she first had sex, she told me about it. I asked for details, but she said I will find out on my own.

Before we got to high school, Yellow had lots of practice with sex. I think she was good at it. Yellow practiced sex a lot and told me every single time that she did. I admired her confidence when she talked to boys. She commanded their attention, even our male teachers. When we had to stay extra hours for tutoring, Yellow did not have to. She always had an excuse that the teachers accepted. She would always have someone waiting for her outside of the school building.

Some days, she even had grown men pick her up. In Liberia, we call them *big papay* dem. The Big papay dem are usually older married men with well-paying jobs that preyed on younger girls. They used to wait patiently in their big cars for Yellow. Yellow had that kind of effect on them. Each man had a juicy story that she would share with me. Although most of the stories ended with Yellow saying, "They all jeh want sex. Dah all. Nothin' big." She gave them sex and they gave her flashy things.

As for me, and my fire-coal self, I did not stand a chance in that sex world. What could I offer? I'd tried to get Alfred, one of the boys on the football team, to kiss me at our back-to-school Jam, but that turned out really bad. I was soon known as "Black snail". The whole football team found out about my failed kiss. *Black snail* followed me all through grade school. I had practiced kissing many times in the mirror prior to the incident. I was sure Alfred liked me because he was always mean to me when his friends were around but nice in secret. This was a sign. I saw it on American TV shows.

Alfred walked me home several times and we talked about his problems at home. He shared some of his art with me and told me that if his parents would allow, he would pursue art. He was quite good with just a pencil and sometimes oil paint. He hated school and math, but his dad said after high school he was going to the engineering college in Harper. Harper is the most southeastern part of Liberia. The trip there would take at least a day on the terrible red dirt roads covered with the dust during the dry seasons and thick muds when it rained. I worried about him going that far, but parents always had the final say.

At school one day, I caught Alfred looking under my uniform skirt as I was bent over to pick up my pen. When our eyes met, he smiled and looked away. All the things Yellow told me about men and the signs from the TV were there. I knew he was just shy but actually had a thing for me. On the morning of the kissing incident, I ironed my uniform, wore a new black stretchy headband, rubbed some Vaseline on my shoes to get that new shine and hurried to school. I got to school a little earlier than usual so I could sit in the hallway and catch everyone scrolling in.

I knew Alfred came to school early because his mother worked at the bank and had to drop him off, before her work that started at 8am. Two days prior to that morning, Alfred walked me home and squeezed my butt before we parted ways. At first, I was shocked, but this was the last sign I needed to make my move.

Yellow and I laughed about the butt squeezed. 'If la me, I way make my move na na. He ready." She told me in Civics class.

I put peppermint candy in my mouth as I waited in the hallway of the school- watching students walk in.

Fine Bright Geh

When I saw Alfred come in, I stood up so he could see me and make eye contact. As our eyes met, I slowly made my way through the sea of students in their blue and white uniforms. I kept telling myself Alfred wanted me, but was just too shy to show it. So, with Yellow's boost of confidence, it was time to show him that I also wanted him. I made my way to him and stuck out my tongue while motioning him for a kiss. Alfred stood there with a look of disgust on his face and my lips were still pushed out like a fool.

At that moment, the Black Snail name was born. Alfred did not say anything to me. A few people standing around (including his friends) laughed as I just stood there with tears forming in my eyes. I needed the strength of a dump truck to drag me, and my embarrassing lips, out of that hallway. I left thinking this could never happen to Yellow. She had kissed so many guys in that same hallway. In fact, she's even broken up another relationship with a kiss in that very hallway. I do not know what spell Yellow had guys under, but I knew I did not have it. I was just the Black Snail.

One of the big papay dem Yellow use to date had a daughter that attended the school right behind ours. It was a government school. The teachers at government institutions were usually on strike because of salary delays. I used to envy the students sometimes because they were always outside where the street vendors hung out, while we were stuck inside with our lessons.

The big papay's daughter came to our school one afternoon to fuss with Yellow and warn her about seeing her dad. She made such a big scene and everyone could hear her calling Yellow bad names. I stood there next to her, embarrassed, but glad I was there with my friend.

The girl said, "You and dah darkness you call a friend are lucky."

Somehow, in the middle of Yellow's mess, my skin made its way into the conversation. People could not talk about me without dragging my skin color into it. As the crowd got bigger, I managed to step away to wave down a motorbike to leave the scene. I got Yellow to leave with me although, all the noise, did not seem to bother her. As we drove off holding on to the pehn-pehn boy, she requested we stop by the supermarket for some cheese balls. Cheeseballs were her favorite thing. It always cheered her up.

Yellow and I had a routine most weekdays after school. If one of her many men did not pick her up, we took a transportation motorbike to meet them wherever they were. We will make a stop at the supermarket and get cheeseballs as we make our way to meet Yellow's guest.

While at the guesthouse or hotel, I would sit outside while she went into a room with her lovers. I usually did my homework during this time or just walked around the area to keep myself busy. When Yellow and whichever guy came out of the room, we headed home together. She told me all about what she did inside the room with these guys. I always wished I was in her place with all the attention and money she got for being in those rooms. Yellow shared her money with me, but I wished I could feel what she felt. I wanted so much to be her.

At school, when everyone talked about Yellow and her relationship with men, she was unbothered. I was the only one that got dragged into it with names like *'Yellow policeman'* and the *'sex bodyguard for Yellow'*.

In fact, every drama, and trust me she had a lot, Yellow was involved with, my name was in it too. That time when she kissed Benatta's boyfriend, I got called "ugly like sin" just for being there. When Yellow stole my notes to spy during a test, I got graded zero while she stayed to make up the test.

"Why you let her take your notes?" Monsieur Fred, the French teacher asked.

Fine Bright Geh

People called me stupid for letting Yellow get away with all this. "They did not know real friendship," I would tell myself. People just didn't like Yellow and that was not her fault. She was my *fine bright friend*.

We never really got into disagreements until she went into a room with Alfred. The same Alfred who I wanted to kiss and it turned into the Black Snail saga. Yellow had sex with Alfred and she said she was paying him back for what he did to me. I could not believe it even after we pulled up to his house one afternoon for Yellow to teach him this lesson. I was hurt sitting outside near Alfred's mother's Nissan Sunny waiting for them to do their business.

"What is it about her that he chose over me?" I wondered. He had invited her to his house after school and she accepted. "Why her? I mean besides her lighter skin, she was short, not smart and could have anyone, so why did she have to say yes to Alfred?" It was hard to accept she did this for me.

When I got home that evening, I told my Aunt Tata what Yellow had done. My Aunt said maybe it was time to get boys to notice me so I could stop following Yellow. She said maybe I was too dark that's why nobody noticed me. I was confused because if it was about skin, Alfred was also as dark as or even darker than me. Nothing made sense about her rationale. I did not understand it, but I wanted to make sense of it because I still wanted Alfred. I wished he would see that I was a better option. If he could get past my skin, I was better than Yellow. I had to show him.

"It was boring," Yellow told me about her encounter with Alfred.

"Are you sure?" I asked with a tune almost accusing her of lying.

"Trust me, he na even in my top 20. I wor just lying there,-na'ting!"

I didn't believe her. I knew she had her fair share of guys and I had none, but she must have been wrong about my Alfred. He did not look like he was boring. All the sex Yellow had, yet she was never satisfied. She had to go and try my Alfred too.

Her actions took a toll on our friendship. I did not tell her why I was still hurt over her actions with Alfred, even if she said it was for me. I secretly prayed she would feel what I felt for Alfred and then watch someone else take that feeling away. It was not fair that she got everything and everyone and it still was never enough.

Her greed made me hate her. I would sit next to her during lunch, but I no longer helped her with homework. Eventually, I stopped leaving school with her to wait during her sex adventures. Before long, the duo Blackie and Yellow was no more. That was my childhood.

****

In a more recent experience, I had to walk away again from another friend out of betrayal. Although we were close friends who loved each other, he called me Midnight like everyone else. Our friendship started during our refugee days. His name was Amara. He was a math tutor that lived across from our tent in the refugee camp. The Liberian war drove us to Cote d'Ivoire as refugees so we had to make do with that.

Amara was tall with rich, dark skin and very noticeable white teeth; like in toothpaste commercials. He told me he liked white women, like the ones working with the International NGOs, but they all turned him down so he settled for the African ones with light skin. He made it clear that I was not his type because of my dark complexion. We were just friends.

Amara slept with most of the young girls he tutored at the refugee center. It was not a secret. As long as the girl looked bright, she was his type. He used to lie to me about his activities with the girls until I caught him in the act one evening, while spreading my clothes on the grass near his tent. The girl must have been no more than 12 or 13 years old bent over in front of Amara with his pants to his ankles. She was very bright like my old friend Yellow. I even saw a little confidence in her as she walked away from Amara's room without shame, having been caught.

"Uncle Amara, I going oooo." She said as she walked out of his tent.

He stood there embarrassed and tried to explain, but we laughed about it and became close friends after that. He was the only male friend I had at the time. We went to church choir rehearsals together; I shared my food with him and even helped with his laundry, occasionally.

One Sunday after church, we went back to his tent and he made his first move on me. Mind you, we were just friends, but nobody else wanted me. I wanted to refuse him, but I was also afraid to lose my friend. I let Amara have his way with me.

He was rough and rushed to get me naked. I can still remember the dirty white tent blowing back and forth, as he took my virginity away; laying on the NGO issued mattress in the refugee camp.

Ever since my experience with Yellow, I longed for this feeling. Sex was not what it sounded like through Yellow's stories. I felt stupid on that mattress with Amara on top of me making noises and sweating. When we finished, I got up and left like all the little girls he slept with.

The next day was a little unpleasant for me when I saw Amara. He did not bring up what happened so I ignored it too and we went back to being just friends. However, a week after, he asked to do it again and then again and eventually, I was expecting it every Sunday after our church service.

Every time while lying there, I wondered why Yellow kept going back to have sex because it hurt. Amara made cuts and bruises on my private parts after every session. I did not like it, but he was giving me the attention I desperately craved from men. It felt good to be noticed as a darkie. Although Amara was not my boyfriend, it still hurt that he was sleeping with other girls (mostly his students) simultaneously. He said, "It is nothing. Don't worry, it's no big deal". Occasionally, I saw dry semen on his jeans when I washed his clothes, but I was okay because we still had our Sunday sessions.

Amara used to hold my hands in public sometimes even though he said he only liked fine bright girls. I was his exception and that made me feel so good! I used to dress up as some of his bright students would, to get him to realize I could be his actual girlfriend.

"You look stupid with that mehn- take it off," he'll say when I try to wear lipstick for him.

I started to use the cream our church mother was using just to brighten my skin for Amara, but he solemnly took notice. He told me, "That my efforts were attempts at trying too hard". While trying hard for his attention, we missed a few Sunday sessions and then we stopped altogether.

He started to treat me like a stranger. Our friendship faded into my own darkness. I tried to force my way back to his tent a few nights and although he had his way with me, he wanted nothing more to do with me during the day. He would look at me with so much loathe that I started hating myself. I went back to my childhood days of hoping I had powers over men like Yellow did. During one of the night visits, I got pregnant and Amara insisted that I remove it.

"I na teh you I want a baby by a white woman. I nah want no darkie like myself!" he shouted at me.

"You na have to own it; I will take care of it myself." I begged.

Fine Bright Geh

"Yes, but I will be responsible for bringing some kinna darkie to this world."

"It will be my darkie, don't worry."

"You are stupid, wha if you geh papers to travel. Weh you will do wey it?"

"You nah want it. Forget it." I reassured myself.

That was the last time we talked and those were his last words to me. The next morning Amara left Danane and I only heard about him years later when someone posted his photo on Facebook with a RIP hashtag. I felt betrayed when he left me in Danane, but I had to continue with my life.

Still in the refugee camp with my pregnancy, I had hopes of joining a family on the UNHCR resettlement program to the United States. The program took Liberian refugees to America to reunite with their families. Over time, the Resettlement programs became a business. People were selling their spots, taking up fake identities, getting married to their own relatives, all in the name of relocating for a better life.

I stayed in the refugee camp for a few months after having the baby hoping to find a family willing to add me to their program. It was extremely difficult for me as a single mother. It became tedious and hopeless just waiting around for someone to add me, and my baby, to his or her family. I drained all my little resources and in due course, found myself in a taxi at the Liberian-Cote d'Ivoire border heading back home.

When I moved back to Liberia, I had my 8 months old and a little cash to start my life over. Prior to leaving for Liberia, my family and I lost contact because of the war. I spent 7 years in Danane, a small city about 15 miles from the Liberian border. When the war broke, I was in school so I ran with the crowd of people and eventually ended up with strangers that led me to the refugee camp where I had the baby.

Along the way, I stayed with different families throughout my journey over to that refugee camp. Some families were nice and some were not so nice, but one thing they all had in common was discussions about my dark skin. The family I lived with, for a short while in Ganta, said they could not keep me because the pastor of their church said I looked like I practiced witchcraft. I slept in the back of old cars and walked for miles before finding other displaced people to take me in.

The next few years came and went. I completed high school while living in the refugee tent in Danane and ate mostly high protein foods, meant for babies suffering from malnutrition. The World Food Program gave us the food.

My stay in exile involved lots of betrayal and life lessons from people like Amara. I remembered I sold Kala (round pastry made from flour, yeast and sugar) by the roadside just to survive. When I got my daughter, things got difficult so I knew I had to leave to start life in Liberia.

Life in Liberia was a lot different than when I was Yellow's dark friend, but at least I was home. It was hard trying to make a life in a foreign country with a little one. It was already hard for me to get people to like me and now I had a little replica of myself. When some of the girls I knew at the refugee camp made plans to sleep with the INGOs staff or the Ivorian officers, to get some cash for upkeep, I was never good enough for that.

"Nobody wants me," I told myself. "I am too dark even to play a prostitute," that is what stayed with me. The shame of being unwanted kept me off the streets and out of options, which forced me back to Liberia. My move to Liberia was necessary for my survival. I needed to find my family, but I mostly needed a place to lay my head. I could not afford to rent a place so I had to leave.

Back in Liberia, life was nothing like I remembered. Our family house had burned down during the war, the streets seemed smaller, people were not as kind as I recalled, and there were a lot more yellow women. I saw

Fine Bright Geh

giant billboards advertising for women who wanted to be bright. The local markets had so many products to brighten the skin.

"This was my chance to get a new life. Maybe I could join the ranks of fine bright girls while living in Liberia. The whole country seemed like they were trying to be like Yellow. "I na come to the right place." I thought.

I asked around for Yellow when I returned, but was told she also left Liberia during the war. I had lunch with some of our old school mates, but nobody seemed to know Yellow's whereabouts. We laughed about some of the ridiculous things I did in the name of our friendship. I came a long way from being *dark snail*. I did not tell them I still had trouble getting men to like me. I was glad to be home with familiar faces.

After some time, I found someone who knew one of my uncles and his family. Most of them still called me Night or Darkie, but I had accepted it. I had come to carry the shame of my skin around with me. I even stopped using the lightening cream because I saw no progress. In fact, the more I used it, I felt darker and it burned and itched, so I stopped. Maybe I was just too dark or it was not meant to be. I could not get out of the skin I was born into. I figured that there were women darker than I was, but living their lives with so much joy.

"Maybe da na force," I consoled myself.

I just hope my daughter does not grow up and become as dark as me. Right now, she looks like chocolate milk, so I am not too worried. I think when she turns one or two I will start using the cream for her. Maybe an early start will get it to work and she can look like Yellow. I want her to be a fine bright geh. I do not want her to go through what I went through.

Life is not fair, but maybe it gives you a little break when you are bright. At least that is what this world told me.

Big Jue

Her name is Nahsee, but I call her Nana. She was my Nana and I, her 700. She calls me that because that was the last digits of the first cell phone I bought for her. She was so excited when she opened the blue packaging to reveal the Nokia 3310 cell phone. It was a dark blue, square-shaped cellular device with gray buttons. Cellular phones had just made their way to Liberia at the time.

The only company we had was Lone Star Cell, a subsidiary of MTN. The cost of the cheapest phone at the time was about $500 USD. For that price, you got either the Ericsson GA 318 that more or less was big as a house phone or the Nokia 3310 that was more lady-like. I had the Ericsson for about two weeks before switching over to the Nokia. I had to make the switch because it was really heavy, but mostly because I wanted to try the newest toy in town.

Everyone who was someone had to have one of those phones. Cellphones separated the 'Haves' from the 'Denied'. It was the one thing that we certainly didn't know we needed but had to have. What was the point of getting a cellphone if no one else had one? As more and more people started getting cellphones, I made it my duty to secure one for my Nana. She was to me what folks in the West call a sugar baby, but for me, she was so much more than that.

Approaching my 70s, I've come to see age only as an expansion of knowledge and places to visit. Nana brought back a youthful spirit for me and I made it my duty to keep it that way. I remembered our first encounter during the rainy season when my foolish driver Bill splashed into a puddle that drenched the poor girl and her classmates. It was not really Bill's fault, as the potholes on Jallah's Town road were the size of an entire car. Sometimes, I wonder about emergency vehicles on these roads. It was difficult to maneuver the potholes, street vendors, and bikes while driving in Monrovia.

On the other hand, Bill was a reckless driver. All that considered, he was my favorite driver because he kept his mouth shut and his eyes on the road. I could have an orgy in the backseat, and he will drive as if nothing was happening. He spoke only when spoken to and ignored just about everything around him. He mastered the art of minding your business.

As for his driving skills, well that was another story. We had to pay to replace a street vendor table, paint my neighbor's gate and just recently, buy a new keh-keh (motorized three wheeled taxi) for another man. I never argued with those claims because I was aware of Bill's reckless driving. I knew the price I had to pay to keep him around because he held my secrets.

That day, when Bill splashed water on Nana and her girls, I could see the anger on their faces probably insulting us as we drove away. I ordered Bill to stop so that we could apologize. He reversed and put down my window, letting in the splashing rain and exposing me to the group of schoolgirls standing on the side of the road.

Nana stood there with her pink uniform shirt soaking wet and sticking to her body. Her hair was braided neatly back on her neck. She was holding a plastic bag carrying what looked like some books, papers and wore a black pleated skirt.

The water from my Infinity QX 60 truck had really given them a bath. I felt terrible but distracted by Nana's beauty and innocence. The others standing with her were like background noise as I remained fixated on her. I admired the way her uniform hugged her breasts and the definition of the curves through the skirt's pleat. Her innocence was captivating and rare.

The other girls were all around her in the same uniform, but she stood out effortlessly. I felt so bad that Bill had caused her to stand there wet, but I was watching her stand there exposed. I apologized to the angry students with my eyes glued to Nana's chest. She did not speak and was not as angry as the others were. She seemed shy, but I would soon find out that was far from the truth.

I asked Bill to find "something" for the students to compensate for their troubles. "Something" usually means cash as we have learned from our policemen and women. The routine is usually, "fine something for us Papay" which is followed by folded cash, to get out of any traffic violation.

I did not want to travel with too much cash, especially since Liberian dollars (LRD) can be bulky when in large amounts. The dual currency allows me to carry more money with the USD in smaller packages. Because the forex rates fluctuate often, I keep both USD and LRD in the compartment of my cars, in case of emergency. Most times, I just end up using them to purchase calling units for my phone or "something" for police officers.

The day I met Nahsee, I told Bill to give the students a bundle of Liberian dollars, from the front seat compartment, which was the equivalent of $20 USD. Still standing in the rain and crowded around the car, the students all thanked us, but Nahsee said nothing. Our eyes met and she just smiled and looked down at the ground.

As we drove off, the group made their way across the street and I pretended to scold Bill for his reckless driving. I sometimes even threaten to fire him just to motivate him to pay more attention to the road while driving.

We left that day, but Nahsee and her image stayed with me. Her wet face and body tortured me that entire evening into the night. At night, I often requested tea from our live-in Nanny, Binta. She was the same age as our older daughter Nina, who was schooling in Pennsylvania, USA. My wife insisted that we needed another nanny, after the one we had for years, Zoe, had gotten pregnant.

Zoe still worked with us, but only during the day. Binta came at night and slept in the old security quarters. Zoe cooked, cleaned and did most of the housework during the day and Binta was around as the night nanny.

Binta was a young Fula girl from Guinea. She was the daughter of my wife's Tailor. My wife had an obsession with clothes, especially the wax prints we call lappa. She had to sew a couple of new suits every week. Binta's father was her favorite go-to tailor among the others. Everybody knows Liberian tailors always have stories that will let you down when you actually need them, so you can never have just one.

I sat on the porch in my big rattan chair. In my mind's eyes, I wondered about my chance encounter with Nahsee earlier that day. I could still see the number of buttons on her uniform shirt. I remembered the water dripping from the collar of the shirt. I saw how neat her cornrows were, even with the dirty roadside water covering them.

She was a junior high school aged girl, or at least, the age of one of one of my children. I begged my mind to focus on other things. I had a meeting the next morning with a new partner from Taiwan. I wanted to review the contracts, but my mind wanted more of what it saw on the side of Jallah's Town road the previous day. Nahsee was just my type and I knew I could make it happen.

In the few weeks that followed, Bill would search and find Nahsee for me and eventually invite her to lunch at Golden Beach in Sinkor. My heart was racing as she walked towards me sitting at one of the white the plastic tables and colorful beach umbrellas along the ocean. The beauty of being in Monrovia is having easy access to the beach. I wasn't sure why but looking at her walk made me nervous. She certainly not my first, second, nor third younger girl of interest outside of my marriage.

I, like many of my age mates in town, enjoy the company of younger girls. I only started after my older daughter would invite her friends to visit during her high school years. Nina and her friends would have sleepovers at our house and my eyes caught the beauty of her young friends. At first, I was hesitant because I could be their dad, but with time, I convinced myself it was love. I didn't see Nahsee the same way as I saw my daughter Nina. Although I miss Nina after she left for college, to study Political Science at Temple University. I suspected that I missed the desire to be with her friends mostly.

My marriage was one of convenience. I cannot remember the last time I actually made love or climaxed, out of pleasure, with my wife. Two years ago, she decided she wanted to have a baby since Nina was leaving for college in the US. She traveled to Ghana in search of ways to get a "fifty-something" woman pregnant. We have been calling her fifty-something ever since the extravagant 50th birthday boat party in Nigeria six years ago. She ignored her age most days and insulted anyone who dared to bring it up. She was what the kids called NGO- never grow old. Her drive to have children, at an old age, cost us thousands for treatments and transportation back and forth to fertility hospitals in Accra.

"I jeh need your sperm, dah all," she would say to me before our many trips.

I would fly with her, climax into cups in different reproductive and fertility hospitals' bathrooms, all in hopes of getting my wife pregnant. Despite the cost, this method eventually gave my wife what she wanted. After two years of trying and what felt like boatload of semen, the doctors were able to find a way to get my aging wife pregnant.

Right from the onset of the pregnancy, my wife became obsessed with the idea of becoming a mother again and slowly forgot I existed. When the new baby came into the house, she was more consumed with everything else and our relations were just mere convenience. We said hellos and goodbyes and stayed in the same house. That was it!

When Nahsee and I met for lunch, it turned out she was not as shy as I'd imagined. She was confident and highly intelligent. She ordered Malta and sipped through a straw. She spoke softly without any hesitation. Her body looked different in dry clothing. There was no water to expose her curves in her floral dress, but I still saw the outline. She informed me she was running late for her WAEC study session but promised to see me again. Our next meeting was scheduled for the same place, but this time, I brought her a Nokia phone to keep in contact with me.

"I will like to hear your voice every night before I sleep," I said and quickly regretted.

I sounded like a creep. It was strange, how nervous I was, talking to a girl that was still in junior high school. I don't know why, but I really wanted to impress this one.

I gave her some cash along with the cellphone and made another lunch meeting date with her. Cash is king around here, even if it goes against ethics. As I watched Nahsee walk back to the parking lot where Bill was waiting to take her home, she was almost skipping with the happiness of her new phone. I did not walk back with her, as we had to be discrete. I did not like the eyes of other patrons looking at me walking hand-in-hand with Nahsee. I was still a respectable married man even if I just bought new love for the price of a cell phone.

For our third meeting, we went to a different venue. Since people like to volunteer information to my wife, whenever they saw my car at a venue other than my office. My wife was popular within the business community. A few years back, she brought in a container with interior decorations and kitchenware for restaurants in Monrovia. She always had new business ventures and that made her everyone's friend. Sometimes I swear, she had her own band of spies around town. It always amazed me how she knew where I was even in the most remote areas.

My wife was smart, stylish, outspoken, and well off. Sometimes, I wondered how an old, boring, retired auditor ended up with her as a wife. We both got our education in the States, but she spent more time there learning the crazy consumer obsessed culture. Until recently, we only had three children, Kolubah Jr, Mulbah and Nina. The two older boys were settled into their lives in America.

I have never been a fan of life in America because it humbles you in ways that make you appreciate Liberia. Our society gives you rank and people that honor those ranks. For example, we have two nannies, a chef, an errand boy, three security guards at home, one assigned with my wife and the baby, four drivers, and a host of other people constantly reminding us that we are not ordinary people. Not in America.

While there, I worked long hours and fake smiled my way up the corporate ladder. They say America is the great equalizer where everyone is equal and bla bla bla until you are black. I do not miss the fear of driving while black in Philadelphia. I appreciate American opportunities and loathe her life.

As I got to know Nahsee, I started affectionately referring to her as my Nana. I wanted her to experience life outside of Liberia, and I could make that happen. First, we had to establish that she belonged to me. I was past the point of interest with her. I wanted to be in her life permanently. I didn't want any other older guy with a few bucks to cross me on this one. My Nana was special. She made my heart race when she called at night.

"I saved your name as 700 in my phone ooo," she told me the first night we talked.

"Save my name anyway, jeh be calling." I told Nahsee.

I would sit and wait for her calls at night, while drinking my tea under the palava hut (gazebo), with the sounds of my wife and the new baby crying in the distance. Conversations with my Nana was all that mattered. I could do anything for her. Although she was appreciative of every little thing.

Nahsee came from a very humble background. I remembered when I offered to get her an apartment of her own, she refused and later wept with so much joy.

"I nah know what to say seh, 700. Thank you plenty."

She lived with her mother who had way too many children than she could care for. She sold oranges, when they were in season, to help feed her family. I wanted desperately to get my Nana away from that kind of life. She deserved all paid trips with just me, in resorts with bungalows that smelled like a shot of double Black and boxes of cigars. I was ready to give her the world, more than I did with other girls before her.

It was hard to get her away from the noise of poverty and her mother Theresa's ways. Every dollar I gave her, she shared with others. Sometimes on our date, she'll even pack half of her plate to take home for her younger sibling. I had to find a way to get her to stop looking back at that old life of hers.

I convinced Nahsee to let me talk things over with her mother. She was worried at first about her mother finding out that a man of my age and status was interested in her young daughter. Our people will frown on these types of relationships, but with affluence, we got through the meet-and-greet stage quickly. Then, I got her mother a month supply of food and made a plan to get her out of the slum.

Big Jue

I had Bill take the mother to the local market and splurge on her with everything from rice and oil to bath soap and grocery. I contacted my Lebanese business partner to deliver some mattresses that evening to see how serious I was about elevating their lives. My Nana was so happy with my gestures and it made things easier for us to keep seeing each other. I wanted to leave a lasting impression on the entire family so I got some used bikes for some of the siblings and left some cash for them as well.

When it was time to ask permission for Nahsee to move out to her own apartment, to no surprise, I got a resounding yes from the mother. I arranged to start a little grocery shop for the mother. Things were speeding up as I had expected.

In a society with the haves and denied, there was nothing more I could expect. People with the power and money only ask out of courtesy. The answer will often be a resounding yes. I was getting my wish, of moving my Nana to a secluded area where I could spoil her rotten, while her family was slowly moving away from a life of poverty. There was no harm here. Everyone was a winner. At least that is what I told myself to sleep at night.

The mother was lucky enough to have a daughter that caught my eye. I felt obligated to gift her, for such a beautiful gift I got in her daughter. So what if she turned out to be young enough to be my daughter. She was different from all the other little girls I'd been with. This was not like before where I give them things in exchange for sex. I loved Nahsee. She took less from me and gave me so much more.

In all my life, even my entire 37 years of marriage, I had never been this happy with anyone. I could risk it all to make Nahsee into what our society called, Big Jue. I am prepared to get her a well-furnished apartment, the new red Xfinity FX 45, with her own driver that will drive better than Bill, weekly allowances, access passes to the supermarket for weekly grocery, and just about anything a girl could ask for in this town. My Nana deserves a Big Jue status and I was ready to make it happen. "

New Normal

War was something that happened in the movies with Chuck Norris or Jean-Claude Van Damme on the posters. I used to sneak behind the video clubs to watch those movies through the holes in the aluminum zinc. Video clubs were a big deal because who could afford television or VHS?

My mother could barely afford to keep the roof over our heads. My older sister decided to get pregnant again and our one-bedroom could not hold us. I sold boiled eggs during the day and video club peek holes were my only chance to escape my reality.

Sometimes the ticket guys would shoo us away because we were stealing from those who actually paid to see the war movies. I especially enjoy scenes where the hero would set fire on an entire building and walk away slowly with his big gun hanging on his sides, his dark shades, and torn clothing. I wanted to be those guys so badly.

April 6, 1996, I was walking back from the bathroom when I heard the first sound. I had been wetting the bed recently, so my mom made my older sister wake me up at least twice a night to use the bathroom. You ever slept in a wet bed with other people? Let's just say my sister woke up timely, without any hesitation, to ensure no one had accidents. As I stumbled back to our room, trying not to fall over the pots and rubber dishes in the hallway, I heard a loud sound like thunder, followed by a little popping noises. Then, Gardiah, my sister's son, began crying as I entered the room.

We lived in a rented house, which meant rooms on each side of the hallway with a different family in each room. Our rent was only $15 USD a month, but that was more than we could afford. The same sound woke all the other families. We all gathered in the hallway, as the noise and voices, outside got louder.

My mother grabbed Gardiah from the mattress, on the floor and walked outside. My sister wobbled her way out of the room to join the other adults in the hallway. Everyone was talking really loud about packing, but I just wanted to get back to sleep. There was no light outside so I knew it was still my sleeping hours. We had school at 7:30 so whatever this was had to be done before then. The loud popping noise continued and got closer.

"Where's Monconjay, yor start packing!" My mother barked as she walked back into the house.

I was standing in the corner next to our blue drinking water bucket. Water from the well, in the back of our house, was used only for cooking. We had to fill that blue bucket every morning, with water for drinking, from the hand pump. When my sister had Gardiah, we had to use that same bucket for his bath, but Gardiah was now two, so he took baths with me outside in the laundry tub. I drank from that blue bucket so many times, and never noticed the white spots until that night. I stood near it looking at the white spots and imagining a cold cup of water. I was not allowed to drink liquids after 7pm because I would wet the bed. Our mattress was so thin, my urine went right through and unto the floor. I sometimes blamed Gardiah, but he was learning to talk now.

"Monconjay, pack some of our things quick quick," my sister said to me.

"Wettin?" I asked.

"Pack som mon our things, ley shooting."

I am not sure what came over her, but she was moving fast for a pregnant woman. This was her second pregnancy and she usually walks like the fat American man that I saw at the gas station once. That night was different, she moved like a cheetah. She grabbed the drinking water bucket and went outside to the hallway.

I moved to the other side of the room where we kept our clothes in a basket. My mother kept all our church clothes in a wooden chest. The chest had a top and bottom. Gardiah things were in the top and some in a big plastic bag near the table. Gardiah had more clothes because our neighbor gave us her old baby clothes and toys. My clothes were with my mother's and sister's in the rattan basket. We didn't have a lot of clothes, but the tub was always full on wash days.

I hated washdays. The wooden washboards, the hard round soap we called Kabakulu, and cold water always made the skin on my hand peel; and that too I hated it. My mother would yell at me for leaving the soap in the water when I scrubbed the clothes on the washboard.

"If la soap fini, I wey finish you," she'd say, while pointing her fingers at me and placing her other hand on her hip.

I grabbed whatever clothes I could get from the basket. I hurriedly opened the chest to get some of Gardiah's clothes. Then I took the photo taped to the wall. This was the only photo we had. It was a photo of my mother in her "young girl days" as she used to say. She was wearing a black skirt that flares at the bottom and a floral blouse. Her hair was big and stood at attention, but wild and in rich dark color. She looked so happy standing there near a plum tree. The grass around her was unkempt. She was on her University campus in Gbarnga.

"Put them here!" My sister said as she handed me the now empty blue drinking bucket. She dashed to the floor and started rolling the mattress. I threw the photo in first before adding all the clothes on top.

"Wettin you doing?" I asked confused at her actions.

"Gimme the rope mehn" She motioned to the rope on the floor behind the door. She knelt on the folded mattress as she untied the rope to secure the mattress. We used the rope to hang our clothes during wash days, but we had to take the rope down, out of fear that it will be stolen. One of the other families in our house got their rope stolen twice. I was not sure why she was carrying a mattress, but that was our most valuable thing so, I guess I approve of bringing it along.

Outside, the sounds of people talking about packing was soon interrupted with the loudest noise I ever heard, up to that moment in my life. My ears started ringing. I felt my hands shaking. Our mother came to the door yelling for us to get out. Everything else just faded away as we started to walkout out into the night and towards the loud sounds. Yes, towards. The sounds were coming from every direction, so no matter where we went, we were heading towards the noise.

I was crying along with babies and other people. Children were calling for their parents and vice versa. I could actually see the fire in the sky as bullets flew over.

People ran in every direction. It was complete chaos. Although it was still dark, I saw a brown dog running among us. I even saw a chicken crossing, as we got closer to the main road. I was holding my sister's hand with my left hand and the bucket, with our things, in the other hand. My mother carried Gardiah on her back with our mattress on her head. Many people carried their mattresses that same way.

In the group, I saw families from our house, the Fula man with the shop on our corner, Gerry, my classmate and his family, along with the guy my sister said was Gardiah's father. There was no way to prove that he was, so after months of begging him, my mother advised her to let him be.

"Man and woman busney na geh police inside," she used to say to her. "There is no way to show he da father. Only God knows. We will take care of the baby. If la girl, we wey call her Dehcontee (meaning time will tell bor if la boy, then we wey call him Gardiah (meaning new man)."

All the commotion made me want to use the bathroom. I didn't feel well at all and my ears were still ringing from the sound of the guns. We passed by other families going in the direction from which we just came. Nobody seemed to know what was going on. In our group, no one knew where we were going but we had to get there fast.

The bullets were flying overhead in the sky. Then as we crossed the street, the clothing in the bucket kept spilling over so I stopped to push them back in. This was when I saw my first dead body. I think it was a man, as the darkness could not permit me to be sure. I saw a hole in the areas where eyes were and blood all over his face. He must have been wearing a white shirt because it looked red. I remembered he was laying on his back with his hands open as if he was asking a question before he got killed.

My sister jerked her hand from mine and covered her mouth, but she was not fast enough. She had vomited all in her hands by the time we got to the other side of the street. I kept looking at the man lying there on his back with no chance of running away with us. The stupid bucket kept spilling, but I did not try to fix it this time.

My mother adjusted Gardiah on her back and we continued toward Sinkor. The streets were full of confused people. Then, out of nowhere, we saw cars coming with men hanging on them. They were going quite fast through the crowd of people so we all started running to let them through.

My sister grabbed my hands again, but this time tighter. I felt her hand, moist from when she vomited. She pulled me as we ran. A big guy pushed us both out of his way as

New Normal

he ran ahead. I couldn't see my mother and Gardiah, but I assumed we all ran in the same direction. The men on the car seemed cheerful and jubilant. I glanced at them as they drove by. I saw one of them holding a gun in the air.

My slippers flew off my feet so I looked down. Again, there were people laying lifelessly on the sidewalk. I saw a baby crying next to a woman that was shot. She was still alive, but barely moving. People kept pushing and we kept running. The things in our bucket were half now, as things flew out during the run. We kept running until the men in the cars passed.

My sister held her belly and pulled me towards her. We stood on a porch of someone's house along with other people. I could hear babies crying, gun blasting, people yelling for their relatives as the crowd ran in opposite directions. I kept my eyes back for my mother and Gardiah. My sister was looking over too. We both had hoped to see them emerge with the group right behind us. The thing about hope is that it keeps you going. So we did. My sister started yelling out for my mother as we walked behind the group of people. I wanted to wait. I knew my mother couldn't be so far behind. My sister kept pulling me and calling my mother. I heard her voice cracking as she started to cry out with her name.

"Let me go check for her Sista Wleji." I said to her.

She just kept pulling and we kept going. I had yet to see my mother or Gardiah. I didn't know what was ahead, but it started off that way. My sister Wleji and I walked all day until we made it to central Monrovia. Everyone was trying to enter a place called Greystone Compound. I only had pieces of the peanuts that were in my pocket when we stopped. I would sometimes steal peanuts when my mother would boil it to bag it for sale. I sold peanuts in the evenings or when school was out. I wished I'd stolen plenty that day because only a few pieces were carrying me.

My sister was sitting on the sidewalk crying. I was still hopeful that Gardiah and my mother would show up. The crowd at Greystone was hard to infiltrate. We needed to be inside. Greystone was closer to the American Embassy in Mamba Point. People inside were safe. The shootings were not near the Embassy but it was getting closer.

I heard people saying the Americans would send for their citizens. I wondered if we play nice they would take us too? I also wondered why the line was so long. If we stayed any longer at the gates, the shootings will get closer. I yearned to see a face I could recognize. Instead, I saw children my age holding on to their parents and parents fighting their way to the safety reserved for the Americans. I still didn't understand why certain lives matter more than others.

By the end of that day, my sister and I made the sidewalk our bedroom. We spent that and the next couple of nights, in front of Greystone and the American Embassy, hoping that we will get into one of those iron gates. My sister did not want to risk leaving, in hopes of seeing our mother and Gardiah.

At night, we saw bullets fly over like shooting stars and fire in the skies. During the day, we paced around the gates like stray dogs hoping there would be room for us inside. We were not alone, as strangers got together like families. A man who lost his wife and kids kept close to us. He said his name was Papi. My sister talked to him about the cause of the war and what was happening. He told us the rebels didn't shoot in our direction because shooting at the American Embassy meant war with America. I knew from war movies that America had lots of guns. I imagined Chuck Norris fought for America. We could not win them.

The entire area was home to expats and other foreigners, so the war barely showed its ugly face near that area. I bet even the rebels were afraid to mess with chuck Norris guys, I used to think I lost count of the days, but we were wandering around, eating leftover scraps left at the gates, my sister and I joined a group of people taking the brave walk across the bridge in hopes of heading to the border. I heard the adults say things would be better if we could just get to Sierra Leone.

The border between Liberia and Sierra Leone is about a 2 hours' drive from Duala, a commercial district on the outskirts of Monrovia. My sister said we just had to get to there and maybe we could get a ride. If we walked from where we were, we could get to Duala before the evening. She also said there will be a lot of walking, but I was ready for anything that would make me stop sleeping outside on the cold street floor. I missed laying on our mattress, however thin it was. I missed when things were normal.

The day we left the gates of Greystone was a Sunday. I heard the catholic mass service on the radio as we walked, away from the safety of the foreign nationals. We walked in a closed group, hoping nobody get left behind. We passed through Waterside over the "Old Bridge" towards Duala. Waterside market is one of the biggest and usually busiest markets in central Monrovia. But all it had that day was dead bodies under market stalls, trash and lots of bullet shells. As we made our way over the bridge, one could see more bodies floating in the water beneath us.

A little after the bridge was a checkpoint with a few rebels sitting on both sides of the road. I didn't want to continue walking, but my sister and the rest of the group continued with their hands in the air to signify they were just civilians.

"All le men dem, one side, le women dem, one side!" One of the men shouted.

He was wearing his T-shirt around his head with the leg of his jeans rolled up to reveal the knife in his boots. They all looked tired with red eyes and sounded scary with slurred speech.

"If I talk again somebody wey die!" The rebel said approaching the group.

We divided the group and I went to the male side leaving my sister. I kept my eye on her as the men approached us. The one with the t-shirt around his head threw a pack of cigarettes to the other guy. The checkpoint sign, painted in white, was made out of wood and had the letters NPFL (National Patriotic Front of Liberia) in white. There were only four men and our group outnumbered them. They had guns too big for them so it dragged when they walked. They smelled frowsy and wore clothes like mechanics. Their eyes were red and they yelled when they talked. The women were told to drop everything of value and continue.

"Put everything down here," one of them barked.

I kept my eyes on my sister. She put our bucket down slowly but the rebel pushed her away using his gun.

"Keep moving!"

I left the line and ran towards her.

"Where you goin my pekin?" the rebel with the t-shirt on his head asked.

"Please, he small boy, I beg you –please," my sister pleaded.

"Keep going mehn," the one that pushed her with his gun said, pointing it at us.

As we tried to walk away that's when I heard a gunshot up close for the first time. It was so loud. I saw a little bit of smoke coming out of the gun when it fired. Shells rained out of their guns. The rebel with a huge hole in his pants was yelling as he was shooting in the air. I could only hear the ringing in my ears, but he was saying something or maybe he was singing. Most of us fell to the ground with our hands over our heads.

"Don't try me again! I say only le women dem –get up. Go!"

My sister and the other women woke up and started walking away from the checkpoint. I stayed on the ground still scared they will shoot again. I had wet my pants during the shooting. My heart was racing and tears filled my eyes, as they hurried away. The rest of the men stayed on the ground. I looked among them for a familiar face. I soon realized that Papi, who usually stayed close to my sister and

New Normal

I, was not with us that day. I think he made his way into Greystone.

"Yor get up mehn," the rebel that fired in the air said to us.

I wanted to beg him, but he made no eye contact. He had no room on his face for sympathy. He made it clear that we had to stay. He pulled a cigarette from his pocket and asked for matches.

"Pekin, give this matches to la man." The rebel standing next to me said.

I carried the matches, still hoping to beg for my freedom. He took the matchbox from me and said, "Thank you my Pekin.". I stood there feeling the wetness in my pants, still scared I might wet myself again. Then he said, "Go sit down my pekin, you part of us na."

I wanted no part of them. I wanted my sister. I wanted my mother. I wanted to blame Gardiah for wetting the bed. I just wanted a normal life. War movies had lied to me. There was nothing cool about guns or hearing them. The rebels with the guns did not look likes Chuck Norris nor Van Damme. War was a disease that I wanted no part of.

The rest of the men had the same disturbed look on their faces. We awaited our next command from the rebels. This was our new normal. We were to take the identity of rebels and do what they did. We had no families, but ourselves. We had to seize the day with our guns. Life had no rules as long as we had guns in our hands. This was our new normal.

My Owna Kinja (Burden)

We had to push the enemies back. We had to fight to take back our territory before our Generals got word that we had lost control. We stayed up all night exchanging fire in hopes of getting back our territory. If the soldier boys from Guinea made it past the St. Paul's Bridge, then Monrovia was no longer ours.

"Use all ley bullet seh. Just make sure we maintain our territory." One of the Generals said.

On the battlefield, when my arms got tired of shooting, I would lay on the floor or rest against the tires of our unit's pickup truck. We had two pickup trucks assigned to our unit. The main unit was the government militia, but we came to be known as SBU (small boys unit).

We all had our roles in the unit and specific names to go along. I came to be known as Fuck Cat. I got the name graciously from our late general who recruited us, General Barfour. He said my shooting had no pattern to it. "The pekin can just shoot anywhere and anytime. La Fuck Cat there". My other friend, Junior Boy, was called Desperado. He got this name from the movie about a Mexican drug lord. Junior Boy would stand over people and shoot them even after they were dead. He was known for his close-range killings.

Another member of our unit was Joe-the-fucker. "The pekin will fuck any living thing," General Barfour said. "If you give this guy chance, he will fuck dead body seh". We all laughed at the crazy thought but knew it was possible. Every single battlefield was an opportunity for Joe to hump something. I think the drugs made him sexually aggressive. When we smoked, he would run around humping the trees or anyone standing around. We used to laugh at his reaction to the drugs, but he was not alone.

The drugs had an interesting effect even on me. Right after smoking, the ground felt like it was holding me - my feet got heavy. I used to stand in one spot for a long time right after I smoked. Despite the reaction we got from the drugs, we needed it to keep fighting.

My very first encounter with a dead person, I remembered vomiting the entire night. Our main commander at the time told me, "La de first one. Don't worry". The rest of my unit went on to eat that night, but I couldn't, not after seeing that body at close range. I had a hard time even sleeping that night.

The next day was my first introduction to drugs. I needed to get through the day. As we crowded in the back of the pickup truck, General Black gave me tiny little tablets that were wrapped in shining aluminum foil. I took one and passed it along to the others. I was not sure what kind of tablet we were handed, but we all took it- even the others that were not sick. The boy sitting next to me threw his into his mouth and swallowed without any water. I did the same. It was a very tiny pill, but I felt it go down unpleasantly.

After a while, I started sweating and then I forgot I was feeling sick. Everything felt right again. In fact, I felt better than I ever felt. My body became more active and I thought less about my actions. I came to enjoy using my gun. The killing started to feel like I was in a movie or Gameboy. Thanks to those little pills, I felt invincible.

Zuleka Dauda

The Small Boy Unit (SBU) was my family. Charles Taylor was our Pa. I had not met him but so desperately wanted to meet him one day. As it was, only the main generals got to see him. Everyone affectionately called him Papay. They say he had a smooth way of talking that made all the generals eager to fight for him.

Before I was recruited, I only heard about him as the rebel leader that turned President. My father used to listen to the radio in the evenings when we got back from school. There was always talk about the government this, and the government that. It seemed most people had serious issues with the government, especially the police's SOD (Special Operations Unit) and paramilitary's ATUs (Anti-Terrorist Unit). People complained that they stole and raped, but these were the people that I called family, since my real family was long gone in the hassle of the war.

****

I remember the morning of the war as if it was yesterday. I planned to wash my dirty clothes that day. It was early when the guns started overshadowing the regular chicken crowing and Saturday morning routines. We ran with nothing, but the clothes on our backs. In all the running for shelter, I must have followed the wrong family.

Stray bullets flew all over and the shell casings were falling on the streets as we ran for cover in a renovated store in Jallah Town, towards central Monrovia. The lady that was slumped over near my leg, holding tight to her kinja was murmuring a prayer. I don't know why people call a big bundle of anything people usually carried, on their heads, kinja. But I remember looking at the pattern on the lappa of her kinja and the size of it.

Carrying a kinja was a skill in itself. People would wrapped items in a cloth and put them on their heads, skillfully balancing the weight as they walked. They even placed them on top of vehicles to transport to or from distant places- often headed to

My Owna Kinja (Burden)

Monrovia. However, in that room that day, the only kinja we all had to carry, was the fear of dying that hung over us. We all stayed close to family members or each other.

I searched around interminably for my real family. The next few days I would run with others, eat with them, sleep with strangers, and still hope to see someone that I would recognize. I had an older sister and four young siblings. My mother died in childbirth back in Lofa. We moved to the Monrovia only after she died, but life was becoming increasingly difficult for us. My father suggested the younger siblings and I return to Lofa until my sister graduated from high school to help him with our upkeep. Those plans were soon altered with the war.

One night, as I lay in a random building, hoping they did not come to take me away, I was recruited. The pickup with armed men and few boys in regular clothing raided the house in which I sought shelter.

"Weh yor name?"

"Doe."

"Where your people dem?" One of the soldiers asked pointing his gun at me.

"I na know ooo, uncle. I jeh following de people here."

"Whos dat?" He asked pointing to the old man that let me in that night.

"I na know him uncle, I swear! I jeh by myself."

That was all they needed to hear, apparently. For their purposes, I was the only 'able body man' available, so they took me. We drove off as they fired a few rounds in the air.

****

It turned out that guns were loud and heavy. They looked cool when the others were carrying them around, but when I got mine, along with my ammunitions, I wanted to return them. Gun makes everyone equal. I did not feel small holding my AK-47. There was power in that steel. I felt it every time I held it and mostly when I used it.

We learned how to use the guns and we got ammunition for them. They told us that only young boys like myself made up our units. Our only mission as soldiers was to keep our territory protected. We would get more ammunition if we ran out, but we had to keep the Gabriel Tucker Bridge as our side.

If any civilian crossed our path, they were considered a casualty. With those guns in our hands, we could do anything. I remember making older people pump tires just for laughs.

When I was in elementary school, teachers would make us hold our ears and do a squat-like exercise over and again until our knees gave up! It was no fun, but this was pumping tires. With our guns in our hands, we made people pump tires while crossing the bridge and this was our regular entertainment. We had our own assigned pickup, but we hardly ever had gasoline. When we harassed people or sold looted goods and bought gasoline, the older soldiers never let us patrol alone. Being on the bridge was our only mission. It got boring at times. At other times, it left scars I have yet to heal from.

Few weeks before the start of another massive attack on Monrovia, known as World War III, few boys from my unit joined me to walk from the New Bridge towards the Capitol Bypass. Although only a mile or two from where we were usually stationed, it felt good to be patrolling the streets. It would have been much better if we didn't have to carry those heavy guns or walk, but we were in control.

"SBU taking over! I shouted as we walked in the middle of the streets firing into the air.

"Yea, Fuck Cat-nobody na able us," Joe-the Fucker said as he passed me a small pill.

The pill made our walk easy and amusing until we got to the G. W. Gibson, the government school right in the middle of the Bypass.

In front of the government school, was a line of people waiting to enter for shelter. People started running at the sight of us. I was wearing khaki pants with big pocket, brown Timberland boots and a piece cloth around my head. Junior, aka Desperado, wore a militant jacket and jeans with an actual soldier barret on his head. Sometimes, we had to wash the commander's clothing so we stole a few items to make out uniform reflect our power.

Among the crowd, trying to get into the government building was a young woman. She had been taken off the line to be our woman. There was nothing special about her. This is just how things were. We saw someone, we liked them, we took them.

My unit each had their turn right on the sidewalk. We wanted to make her see that we could not be stopped. The streets belonged to us and anyone in it became our property.

When it was my turn to lay on top of her, I did not hesitate.

"Doe, la you der?" she muttered, more out of disbelief than accusation.

"Wha… weh you know me from?"

"La me Alice. I yor sista," she uttered.

My body felt cold. I recognized her! Everything in me, urged me to STOP, but I did not stop. My friends were cheering me on. My gun weighed me down as I pinned my own sister to the cement of the sidewalk. My body was not mine; I felt the motions but only as someone else. It felt as if someone was using my body as I watched from right there. It was me all right, but then again, it wasn't. My mind took images that stay with me to this day.

We left the scene jubilating and recruited two new boys. There were a few casualties left behind, but we had to return to the bridge to continue our mission.

Shortly thereafter, the last of Liberia's bloody wars ended. Our Big Pa, Charles Taylor surrendered, and went into exile. Our unit, like the rest, disbanded; but in the streets, on that floor that day I'd picked up my owna kinja.

It is so heavy. I have never had the courage to lay with another woman recently. I've tried, but my sister's face haunts. Oh, and in the background, are the cheers from my friends. In their cheers, I lost all trace of dignity. In my sister's agony I picked up a kinja that is not going anywhere.

Uncle ECOMOG

Every older man is your uncle, whether he shares relations with your parents or not. Uncle is more of a sign of respect than family ties. You usually get small pocket change from your uncles and they would discipline you when you misbehaved. That was the main role of uncles. I like to think of them as *some-days-good, some-days-bad*.

We have uncles everywhere we turn. Uncles in school, uncles in the stores and shops, uncles at the church and even uncles as strangers. I greet about ten of them just making my way to the hand pump to fetch bath water in the evening. I wished they all gave me more than just a cold 'hello' back when I over zealously waved and called out their names.

"Hello ooo Uncle John," or "Morning Uncle Peter."

Yes, I know their names sounded like what we call 'example names' in Liberia. There were names straight from those NGOs donated textbooks. You know *'There was a boy named John or Peter caught a fish'*. Those names were similar to most of our people around here. We have names like James, Fredrick, Susan, and Mary because freed slaves from the Americas founded our country. At least that is what we

Uncle ECOMOG

learned. One of my real uncles, Unice, used to say Liberians with traditional names are the originators even if some refers to the as country people.

"Country people" is not a term of endearment. There is a huge class system and tribalism in our country. People could tell your identity from your name, but sometimes, folks had both English names and traditional names. You will hear people say, "My name is John Brown, but my country name Torpor."

What happened in those days, African-Americans that were freed slaves returned to Africa to start their own country. Liberia became a place they called home. The native Liberians and the returned Americans had many clashes that would eventually spill into the civil wars.

Some returned Americans took native Liberian children to live with them as indentured servants. Those native children will sometimes have their names changed to reflect the American families that took them in. In fact, some of them willing took on new last names, all in the name of civilization or being kwi.

There are people with 'example names' and indigenous names. We are all still dealing with the situation. So, when I talk about my uncles, I am referring to all of those names; Uncle Peter and Uncle John as well as Uncle Unice, Uncle Tweh, Uncle Blapoh, and even uncle ECOMOG.

ECOMOG was the West African peacekeepers in Liberia after the civil war. They wore army uniforms and rode army cars, so we all called them soldier people. West African countries got together and sent monitoring armed forces to ensure we did not go back to the wartimes.

Although we called ECOMOG soldiers people, I did not think they were soldiers. They didn't go to war and I did not see them fighting the rebels. They were around after the ceasefire agreement with the rebels and the government of Liberia. Their mission was to keep things somewhat normal. I saw them go and I saw them come. They watched soccer with my other uncles, walked around with their small radios playing BBC world service News, bought food from the local markets and gave us some of their packaged food. They were part of our community.

Sometimes I wondered how long they would sit around maintaining peace, but then, I remember how many wars we had. At first, it was just one war in the interior parts of the country. The next war made it to the city and then eventually, we had wars breaking out everywhere. We could not have normal school schedules or anything normal. People were always scared there was another war coming. When we heard even the sound of tires bursting from the main road, we ran for cover. Our lives were a never-ending war show. The older people constantly hovered around their radios hoping for news of some normalcy.

There was this one ECOMOG soldier that I came to like and started calling, Uncle ECOMOG. He was tall and strong and smiled at me when they rode by. When I walked to the hand-pump in the evenings, I could see him sitting under their army green tent. I called most of the other soldiers, soldier man, but uncle ECOMOG was not just any soldier man. He used to stop to talk to me often when he walked through our neighborhood.

I knew him by the mark on his face. He had a deep scar from the corner of his left eye to his cheek. It looked like a picture out of the magazine this white missionary had, with the caption AFRICA on it. The magazine also had a man with spears and a small piece of wood piercing his nose. He had tribal marks covering his face with what looked like a wooden plate sitting in his lips.

I do not know what part of Africa they got those photos from or where uncle ECOMOG got his mark, but it fascinated me. I wanted to know how he got the scars or what they meant. The white missionaries always had photos of Africa that fascinated me. Which part of Africa do they have these people? People around here looked nothing like those in their books.

Uncle ECOMOG

My favorite, Uncle ECOMOG wore his scare with grace. I did not like looking at it at first, as it scared me, but eventually, it grew on me. He was a friendly face compared to those without scars. He made it as if the scar disappeared when he talked to you, just from how nice he was.

ECOMOG soldiers wore those green and black camouflage uniforms that you see in American war movies, where the hero has black lines under both eyes and carried big guns. I loved those movies, but Uncle ECOMOG wore his uniform better. He was always so neat with his uniform freshly ironed. He had a pocketknife hanging on the pocket of his trousers and had shining black boots. On his head, he wore a hard green hat like a motorbike helmet. He never wore any jewelry and always had a small radio with the long antenna sticking out.

I do not remember much of the war, but watching the peacekeepers, reminded me of the anxiety I felt during the wars. I hated when the ECOMOG soldiers would rush by in their army cars, with the red dust following and covering the road. They sat on benches in the back of the pickup with their backs towards each other and their guns pointed at the roadside. Sometimes, I used to wait by the road to see if one of the cars speeding by was carrying uncle ECOMOG so he could smile at me through the dust.

"Joe boy", he'll call out or sometimes just hey!

I liked being recognized that way. I enjoy being a friend of soldiers. Maybe one day I'll be a soldier like him. He was everything a little boy like me dreamt about. He dressed well, had money, car and good morale in the community. I looked up to Uncle ECOMOG. He had a good life. I wanted so much to be like him.

Post-war meant curfew for us, so we had to be home before 7pm. When I would lay in my room at night, I used to hear the army cars go by on patrol and imagine it was Uncle ECOMOG and his friends keeping us safe. I wonder if he was ever scared while out there at night. What if the rebels came back one night while we were asleep and he was patrolling.

Many nights, I prayed for Uncle ECOMOG. I prayed really hard. My mother used to yell and make babbling noises when she prayed, but I just spoke quietly to God to protect uncle ECOMOG and keep him around. I doubt God heard me since I didn't make loud noises, but I prayed anyway.

On a Saturday, I was walking back from buying kerosene for our lantern when I ran into uncle ECOMOG and my uncle Unice playing checkers under the shade of the guava tree. Uncle ECOMOG was focused on the board but looked up when I greeted them.

"Joe boy! Come and say bye," he motioned to me.

I walked towards them even though I did not understand what he meant by the 'bye'. December sun was no joke. I was glad to be called under the shade of the tree. His news was not as pleasant as the breeze hitting my face.

"I will be going back to Nigeria soon. Take care of yourself big boy!" He said with a smile that made his facial scar croaked.

He reached over and rubbed my back in a circular motion and continued to play his game of checkers. Uncle Unice kept his eyes on this bright green and yellow board with bottle caps as seeds. He told me to give his regards to the "big belleh" and tell her he will stop by before curfew. My mother was pregnant and that had become her name; big belleh or big belly.

Sometimes you got names just from the strangest things. We called the lady that sells fish, fish woman. That was her name. Everyone just said hello ooo fish woman. The kerosene boys were called just that, Kerosene boys. It was no surprise that people greeted my mother with big belleh or the kids sang, big belleh where the baby, as she walked by. We love to give our own names to people. It was just what we did.

Uncle ECOMOG

My walk home after the news from uncle ECOMOG was a long, sad, one with the sun beating down on me. I did not want him to leave. I was not sure how far Nigeria was from us, but I knew he could not protect us from there. Africa was a very big place. Our little country, of barely a little over 4 million people, is big enough that people right the capital Monrovia are oblivious to things happening in the other 15 counties. Similarly, wars in other countries were not on our radar. So, even if Uncle ECOMOG moved the county, that was too far for us in Monrovia.

I knew they said the war was partly over, but there were still armed robbers he needed to protect us from. A few weeks prior, some of the soldiers shot a guy that tried to break into the rice store in the big market. They said he climbed into the ceiling and waited until the business day was over. He was locked into the store, so at night, he tried to breakout. In the process of making his way out of the locked store, he was caught.

Everyone was talking about it and how desperate the thieves were to do such a thing. The patience of a desperate thief to wait all day and night was a scary thought for us. Who would protect us from guys like these if uncle ECOMOG left?

I got home after saying bye to Uncle ECOMOG to find my pregnant mother lying flat on the floor crying her eyes out. She does this thing where she cried with her hands on her head like they do when we went to funerals. I hated seeing that. People would cry out loud and out of control. The last funeral I attended was my mother's mother. My mother had a whole performance on the ground with several people holding her back throughout the day from rolling in the dirt. My grandmother died from illnesses. She had this cough that sounded like a rocket launching, when she coughed. All of us children would cover our ears when she coughed and call it GYC (grave-yard cough) behind her back.

With my mother's dramatic cry at the funeral, they stopped the funeral processions several times to give her time to let out her loud cries while rolling on the church floor. At the end of the day, she looked like a mechanic from the bike shops. The family insisted on wearing white with purple head wraps for the women.

At home that evening, my mother was crying uncontrollably with her older sister who was sitting on a stool next to her, rubbing her back in a circular motion. People like to rub your back when you are in pain. I guess it is supposed to make you feel better. I wish it transferred the pain, but I doubt it. Instead, I watched my mother on the floor wearing only a lappa being consoled by her sister's useless rubbing of the back.

"I na do it, Sta' Etta," my mother said to her sister.

"I finish ooo. I na die- yor beg my husband for me ooo," she continued.

I walked past them and went into my father's study to pour the kerosene in the lantern before the dark came. My mother's crying followed me as I walked inside with her cracked voice trying to explain through the tears that she did not do it and whatever "it" was, it had to be explained to my father because she was not leaving. She begged her sister to plead on her behalf.

Often times, older people would call others to help work through their quarrel [plawor as we say]. Children were not allowed in the room when the adults made plawor. In fact, when adults talked, we knew our place was away from their discussion.

"You nah see big people talking here? Yor go outside mehn!" They often scolded.

My father's study was always dark and smelled like kerosene. He spent most of his evenings and nights in there. It was more of an old guest room that he added a bookshelf in, than an actual study. The window was tiny so he always needed extra light, even during the day. The floors had a floor mat that looked like a checkerboard. The desk he worked on was an old table that used to sit in our outside kitchen.

He insisted that we called this space his office and stayed out of it while he worked. He said he was working on a book about the Liberian civil war. His plan was to complete the book and send it to his little brother, my uncle Tweh that lived in England to help him publish it.

Uncle Tweh left Liberia as a little boy to live with a missionary and his family. My father always said his brother would one day return, but we had yet to see him. My father stayed to himself most days. He was a very smart man, but conservative or as the adults would say 'stuck in his ways'.

I walked back out of the study with the empty kerosene container and heard my Aunty Etta say.

"Bor why you let dah man come here. Why mehn?" her voice sounded like she was making an accusation.

Through her sobs, I heard my mother repeatedly say, "I nah do it Sta' Etta. I beg you talk to him for me. I na do it."

It was painful to ignore my mother as she cried. I knew better than to get involved in big people things. My mother's pregnancy made her struggle to get around in the last few months. She could barely reach the top shelve for the seasonings when she cooked.

Her sister, Aunty Etta had to come live with us to help with the cooking and cleaning until she was no longer pregnant. They always did that for each other. Aunty Etta used to tell me how my mother's stomach was so huge when I was in it. When Aunty Etta got pregnant, my mother left our house for a few months too. When my mother was not pregnant, we only heard from Aunty Etta when she had troubles with her husband. She was usually the peacemaker, but sometimes she came to my parents in tears.

My mother sat on the floor carrying her load, as the people say. "If you get pregnant, you will carry your own load" was the warning my older cousins used to get. My mother only had boys, but a few of my cousins stayed with us. I could not imagine her pain sitting on that floor.

Through her tears, she was breathing heavily. Her belly had her looking darker, swollen, and almost not my mother. I hated how she looked, but it was worse when she cried. I was sad listening to her sobbing and begging the peacemaker to talk to my father on her behalf.

The sun went down and the evening breeze made its way to our house. My father made his way out of the study and unto our veranda. I sat a few yards from the house under the plum tree pretending to be cleaning the lantern shade. We had two big lanterns for the living room that constantly had black smoke that my mother complained about. I used the opportunity of cleaning the shade to listen in on my mother's crying.

Aunty Etta tried to talk to my father in a low monotone voice, "I beg you, we gah to talk ley thing here."

He shouted back so even our neighbors could hear, "Talk wuttin Etta"

"I beg you papa," Aunt Etta pleaded.

"Nothing to talk mehn Etta. Your sister slept with la ECOMOG. Let her leave my house. Maybe la his belly. I na stupid," he said before walking back into the house.

When I heard the door of his office close, I walked back towards the house holding the lanterns. I was not sure how long their fight was going to last or which ECOMOG he was referring to, but it changed things for me. I went to bed that night hoping the ECOMOG that went to bed with my mother was my Uncle ECOMOG. I imagined my mother packing her things and traveling back to Nigeria with him. I knew she would take me along with them. They had to. What if he was my real father?

About the Author

Zuleka is a Liberian living and schooling in the Virginia, USA. She holds a Master's in Education and currently a doctoral student in Planning, Governance and Globalization with focus on Africa and representation of Africans.

Along with a diverse group of writers from online communities across the world, she authored her first book, *Better Than IRL* in 2019.

Zuleka strives to have her stories as vibrant as her headwraps. She believes through stories we can change the narrative of Africa.

She can be found online at

*IG: @ Zuleka_*

Twitter: Zulekatweets

Made in the USA
Columbia, SC
06 April 2021